Stumbling into Trouble

By

Bill Greco

KCM PUBLISHING
A DIVISION OF KCM DIGITAL MEDIA, LLC

CREDITS

Stumbling into Trouble by William Greco

ISBN-13: 978-1-939961-96-9
ISBN-10: 1-939961-96-3

First Edition

Publisher: Michael Fabiano
KCM Publishing
www.kcmpublishing.com

This book is dedicated to all of us who love our animals; especially the greatest animal lover I know, my wife, Laurie.

Sometimes it's only through our animals that we experience life's greatest gift of all – unconditional love.

Contents

Preface

My story of Lucy is fiction, Lucy is not. My wife and I found her on Petfinder. We did have to wait and found ourselves e-mailing the rescue. We were hoping for Faith, her beige and white sister. The young lady from GROWL, an animal rescue based in Rockland County, New York brought us Lucy instead.

Melanie is our failed attempt at fostering. We fostered her for Have-A-Heart Rescue, based in New Brunswick, New Jersey, for ten days and were unable to part with her. Lucy and Melanie were both found on www.petfinder.com, an Internet site devoted to rescuing dogs and finding their forever homes. This excerpt from the website explains their mission:

"Petfinder is an online, searchable database of animals that need homes. It is also a directory of more than 13,000 animal shelters and adoption organizations across the U.S., Canada and Mexico. Organizations maintain their own home pages and available-pet databases."

Our mission

To use internet technology and the resources it can generate to:

1. Increase public awareness of the availability of high-quality adoptable pets
2. Increase the overall effectiveness of pet adoption programs across North America to the extent that the euthanasia of adoptable pets is eliminated
3. Elevate the status of pets to that of a family member

From the comfort of their personal computers, pet lovers can search for a pet that best matches their needs. They can then reference a shelter's web page and discover what services it offers. Petfinder also includes classified ads, discussion forums and a library of animal welfare articles."

Lucy was initially named Hope. She continues to give us love and hope and as this story tells, she indeed did save us. Melanie is our newest rescue, a tan fifty- pound terrier with scruffy wire hair. She is an adorable klutz; I hope you will like Lucy's and Melanie's adventures and future frolics.

Stumbling into Trouble

Part I
Dumb Dog

Chapter 1

Ben sat on the cold steps of the animal hospital. His eyes blurred by tears as his mind raced with thoughts of hopelessness and dread. Lucy, his princess of a dog lay on the precipice, teetering on the fine line between life and death. Melanie his other rescue mutt was lost somewhere in the Ramapo Mountains. His life was collapsing around him. His girlfriend abandoned him, his finances where in shambles; he was beaten, jailed, and nearly killed. Events pushed his spirits down the depths of self-pity. His only hope clung to the small chance Lucy would survive her wounds. In his despair, Ben tried to piece together the events that led him to this time and place. He looked back at a happy beginning. It was a sea-shore vacation that unraveled the threads of his life. It led him to these cold stairs and a bleak, dismal future. He sat trying to comprehend it all. Bens mind raced, "how ironic it is that a little puppy named Hope led me to this hopeless end," as he reviewed the sequence of events responsible for all his misery.

Traffic was backed up on Route 1, all the way to the beach. Ben's mind wandered as he stared at the empty lane of oncoming traffic. It was a beautiful, hot summer day. The car's thermometer read 85 degrees, but he knew the temperature was going up to a sweltering high of 94 degrees. The sun was glaring down on his windshield. It appeared as if no one was leaving the beaches. To his agitation, it seemed as if every vacationer in the country was on Route 1 heading to the beach. The empty pavement to his left shimmered with the mirage of water as the heat rose like wisps of steam from the baking black-top. Cars were stacked bumper to bumper all the way to the sought-after shore beaches everyone craved. Progress was now measured in car lengths rather than miles. Ben's mind wandered to thoughts of his current girlfriend, Sandy. He felt a knot in his stomach as he considered his current relationship. He was hoping the condo he rented would be clean, knowing his girlfriend was going to be there with her usual critical eye. He wondered why she was so hard to please. Ben prided himself as a man of simple needs who always made the best of any circumstance he found himself in. Sandy was his opposite, critical of everything and anything that crossed her path. He hated whenever he found himself dwelling on the deterioration of the relationship.

Ben sat yearning for the Sandy he had met. On their first date, he recalled how nervous he was as he walked down the stone path to her house. The house was large and spoke of money. There was a warm light in every visible window and he observed an elegant décor in the spacious rooms that were visible through the curtains. His heart raced and his palms became sweaty as he approached the front door. Wild thoughts ran in his head as his fight or flight instincts kicked in. "I must be crazy to think this girl will be interested in me," he thought, "I should just turn around and head back home." He wondered how he could ever be interesting enough to someone so obviously wealthy since he had little to offer. Ben handled millions of dollars of other people's money; he owned a modest home in the burbs and made a comfortable living. Staring at the palatial home of the girl he met at the mall, he knew she was in the upper stratosphere of society, a far cry from his mundane life. Ben stood at the door pondering the inequalities of their lives and rather than turn and run he mustered the courage to ring her bell. "What the hell; what do I have to lose?" he mused as the housekeeper opened the door and invited him into the marble-floored foyer. He gazed up at the oak staircase to an upper terrace and farther up to the largest chandelier he had ever seen in a home. "Holy crap," flashed in his head, "this looks like a catering hall." Sandy appeared at the top of the stairs. Her blond hair caressed her shoulders accenting a rhine-stone garnished V-neck top. She had on a pair of hip-hugging jeans and a gold link belt. Her shirt was just short enough to play peek-a-boo with a belly button stud. She was petite and shapely. Images of the belle of the ball making her grand entrance at the top of a cascading staircase popped into Ben's mind. Smiling, she hurried down the stairs. Grabbing his arm, she pulled him towards the door.

"Let's go before my father comes to interrogate you; he can be such an ass," she said as they hustled out the door. She practically dragged him to his car. He lost his nervousness in the rush, and once in the car, her warm, inviting smile melted all the doubts he had.

"Well, let's go. What treats do you have in store for me on our first date?" Sandy said in an expectant tone. Sandy excitedly told Ben about the new Vera Wang bag she found in a quaint shop in Manhattan. He listened intently with an air of excitement as she scooted closer to him and ran her fingers over the hair on his arm. Ben pulled up to a small mom-and-pop Italian restaurant he frequented. It had an at-home, relaxed atmosphere. The waiter was the couple's son who also doubled as a busboy. The father was the bartender and maître de, and mom was head cook and bottle washer. Ben and Sandy ordered ravioli, the hand-made specialty of mom, and a delightful bottle of Chianti. Ben felt the night was magical. They laughed and exchanged stories. She was relaxed and opened up to him about her overbearing father and his disappointment in her. She was open and dropped any pretenses she might have brought to the table, and Ben felt an immediate connection to her. They both spoke so easily and openly about their lives that Ben felt he could tell her anything. The wine and the food made its magic as if it were the scene from *Lady and the Tramp*. They soon found themselves at Ben's home. She loved Ben's humble surroundings and delighted in his simple, clean décor. They caressed and stripped as they made their way to his master bedroom. Ben was amazed at the comfortable and uninhibited lovemaking. It was a new experience for him. There was none of the awkward fumbling or second thoughts, and they fell into a natural rhythm that felt as right as it felt good. Afterward, they lay contemplating the night's enchantment and chatted about the fun they had until they drifted off to sleep. Ben awoke with Sandy's hand draped across his chest and her head on his shoulder. He had never felt anything could be this right. He lay happily, thinking this could be the soulmate so many talked about.

It was only a couple of whirlwind weeks later that Sandy moved into Ben's house. Ben was able to talk so easily to Sandy, and the sex was great. She had the bad habit of a girl raised in an affluent household – she loved to shop and spend money. Ben was not well received by Sandy's father. Her father disapproved of her living with Ben, and Ben had the impression that he felt Sandy was dating below her station. Sandy and her father argued whenever they stopped by her father's house. Often he would call to complain about a bill he received from one of Sandy's many shopping binges. Sandy grew very moody and upset as a result of the constant fighting with her father, and it started to spill into her relationship with Ben. Ben was panicked that their free and easy relationship was cooling. Her father cut off her support after a massive blowout at their home. Ben felt responsible for her father's disapproval. He allowed her to use his credit cards and checking account to pacify her dark mood. Shopping was Sandy's cocaine; it gave her a high. Ben became Sandy's facilitator, satiating her shopping habit to keep her in an amicable mood. The relationship deteriorated into a one-sided affair. Ben, craving her attention and affection, did everything he could to improve her mood. With all his efforts, he received little in return. The magic was waning, and Ben felt himself slipping into a depression that seemed to taint every aspect of his life. He continued to throw money at Sandy, for he did not know what else to do. Her spending kept their social interaction alive through the numerous discussions of her day shopping and her modeling the clothes and accessories she had purchased. It kept Ben amused for a while, but the emptiness of the relationship continued to undermine his confidence. Ben knew deep down that he was only fooling himself to think he had a stable relationship with Sandy.

Chapter 2

The affair reached new lows, but as time progressed a small miracle happened. The miracle was his dogs, Lucy first and then Melanie. Ben's affection and attention turned to "his girls." He found a new reason to get up every morning. He walked, cared for, pampered, and talked to his dogs. Sandy became a second thought. He no longer had time to stress about the lack of attention from Sandy, he had his dogs. They greeted and showed him love every day. His dogs kept him company on his walks and sat with him when he watched television. Sandy was free to do as she wished.

The bumper-to-bumper traffic snapped Ben's mind back to the road. The thoughts of Sandy and the constant whoosh of air from the car's air conditioner were starting to annoy Ben. No matter how loud he made the radio, he couldn't drown the noise of the air or the thoughts in his head. Ben kept daydreaming and seemed hypnotized by the flashing brake lights and the constant stop and go. He knew he should have left two hours earlier but he had been unwilling to sacrifice the extra sleep.

Ben Grece sat knowing the last half hour of his commute would now take over two hours. He was passing the Dover Air Force Base on Route 1, the only two-lane road leading to the Delaware beaches. It was a typical Friday commute to the beach. Cars with packed roof racks, kayaks, loaded bicycle carriers, and back seats stacked with suitcases, bags, and children inched their way along. In Ben's back seat sat his two rescue dogs. Lucy was a jet-black spaniel mix and his latest rescue, Melanie, was a beige and white terrier mix. Melanie was already drooling profusely; Ben had taken the precaution of laying several towels over the rear seat. The unfortunate puppy had a severe case of motion sickness. The condition would progress from excessive drooling to gagging on her drool and would culminate in a round of vomiting. Ben felt sorry for her travel affliction. Lucy was not as compassionate. Lucy moved to the opposite side of the rear seat. There she looked out the window, fascinated with the surrounding farmland and scanning for animals running in the fields. After passing Dover, cornfields grew on both sides of the one-lane road dotted with an occasional farm stand or garden center. Lucy's occasional furtive glances at Melanie would be to check on her hurl status to make sure she was out of range. Once Melanie vomited, Lucy would jump into the front passenger seat and refuse to move. Who could blame her? It was not a pretty sight. The stop-and-go was taking its toll. Despite the Dramamine, Ben gave her before leaving his home, the gagging phase started. Lucy stared intently at Melanie, ready to make her move to the front seat. Lucy sprang forward just as Melanie began to vomit. Ben thought he could hear Lucy saying, "There she blows."

Melanie came to Ben as a result of his attempt to provide a foster home for dogs. A close friend of Ben's, Melissa, runs Have Some Heart dog rescue in New Brunswick, New Jersey. She was stuck with Melanie when a family that was adopting her unexpectedly backed out. Melissa was leaving for a vacation in Florida the following day and asked Ben if he could foster the pup for ten days, Ben thought he could help. He received approval from her for the foster care. Ben and Lucy were off to South Jersey to pick up the pup. Ben should have known Melanie had issues when Melissa informed him that she had just bathed the dog he was to pick up. Melissa told him she may still smell of vomit. On the way back to Montvale, Ben's hometown, Melanie christened the rear seat of his car with a fresh round of vomiting.

Melanie was a straggly, semi-wire-hair terrier mix. She was beige with a white snout, a white diamond between her eyes, a white chest and shoulders, white paws, and a white tip of her tail. Melanie looks like Sandy from the play *Annie*. She has a slow, waddling gait and often appears awkward and clumsy. Her paws are too big for her body and frequently cause her to trip. Melanie was a dorky, clumsy, and needy pup. Ben set up a crate for her bed and had the kitchen and living room puppy-proofed and ready. Ben carried his new addition into the house and placed her in her crate on the soft bed he had placed inside. She sniffed the bedding and the air of the crate. Sandy walked into the room with arms crossed and her trademark scowl on her face.

"Well, at least she's cute. I hope you don't expect me to take care of it."

"The dog is a temporary guest; I'll take care of her," Ben said.

Ben handed Melanie a rawhide roll he had in the crate for her. The cute puppy snatched the treat greedily in her teeth. "Easy girl," Ben reprimanded her as he attempted to take the treat back. Melanie rolled her upper lip up flashing a beautiful set of pearly white puppy teeth. Ben was not impressed and did not like the aggression Melanie was exhibiting.

"Okay, keep the bone this time, but that will have to stop young lady," he joked to the dog. "Maybe she has distemper or rabies," Sandy added.

"No, she's had all her shots; she just has had a rough upbringing. With a lot of love and attention, she'll be fine. Besides we only have her for ten days."

"I hope so. That dog looks vicious, keep it away from me," Sandy added.

Ben ignored Sandy's comments and tried to pet his young ward, which once again showed him her teeth. Melanie was furiously chewing the rawhide and dropped it for a second when Lucy barked. Ben quickly snatched the treat back. Melanie, as if a switch was flipped, returned to the happy, playful pup he first met. She flopped and played with Lucy and Ben as if the event never happened. She was an adorable klutz, tripping on her own feet or the toys Ben had bought for her. Even Sandy started to warm up to the new pup – until she squatted mid-play and peed on the floor.

"Oh my, Ben, clean that up. The whole house is going to smell of pee."

Ben cleaned the small mess; it was an expected issue with a new pup. Ben prepared Lucy's and the pup's food. When he placed the food down, Melanie ran to her dish; Lucy's dish was next to hers, and the pup again showed teeth and growled when Lucy approached her food. Ben reached to move the puppy's dish away from Lucy's, and Melanie hoggishly wrapped her paws around the bowl and growled at Ben. He gingerly slid Lucy's bowl over and away from the pup. Once the food was finished, Melanie Hyde returned to Melanie Jekyll, and the lovable pup reappeared. Ben wanted to give Melanie some treats to chew but treats transformed this lovable pup into a snarling and growling beast until she consumed them. Sandy was ready to send Melanie back. Ben reminded her they had committed to watching her for ten days and it looked like it would be a long ten.

Ben had a big day of growling and cleaning up the little messes. Melanie refused to recognize the concept of outside and refused to walk on a leash. Ben locked Melanie in her crate for the night and covered it with a towel so she would sleep. Ben and Sandy were halfway up the stairs to the bedroom when the crying started.

"Oh God, will that dog whine all night?" Sandy asked.

"Ignore her. She'll stop when she gets tired," Ben told Sandy.

The whining and whimpering progressed into high shrill barks. After an hour of non-stop crying and barking, Ben and Sandy had had enough. Ben went downstairs and placed a radio with soothing music near Melanie; she stopped crying and wiggled at the cage door when she saw Ben. Radio playing, Ben retired back to bed. No sooner did he leave the room when Melanie started barking again. Entering the bedroom, Sandy started to whine also. "I need to get some sleep. You have to shut that dog up."

Ben just turned and walked back down to the living room. He spread out a blanket next to the cage and Melanie quieted. Ben dozed on the hard floor, and each time his eyes closed, Melanie started to whine.

"She wants me awake. Sleeping on the uncomfortable floor isn't good enough for this mutt," Ben thought.

It was a sleepless night. With daylight, came a repeat of the previous day's events. Ben was working from home, but the pup could not bear to be left alone. She showed teeth and growled over her possessions and food.

"Take the beast to the pound," Sandy argued to Ben.

"She's possessive; it must be from the pound she came from. It'll get better, be patient," Ben said.

By the third day of no sleep and non-stop whining and growling, Ben had had enough. Lucy sensed his frustration and took over. Lucy eyed Melanie wearily.

Lucy treated Melanie as a mother would treat a misbehaving child. She inserted herself between Melanie and Ben. If she growled, Lucy would scold Melanie and block access to her treats or food until Melanie submitted to her. If Melanie showed teeth, Lucy would nip the growling pup, forcing her to lie and roll on her back before Lucy would allow her to eat. Lucy slept by Melanie's cage, forgoing her own bed to lick and comfort Mel until she fell asleep. Witnessing Lucy at work was terrific. By the sixth day, Melanie would sleep the night and no longer showed her teeth near food or bones. She even started doing her business outside without an accident after a week. Lucy, in her mothering role, found new vitality. She seemed to enjoy the responsibility. When the day came to return Melanie, Ben did not have the heart to break up the two. Melanie followed Lucy pie-eyed everywhere. Lucy taught her how to be a good dog and in the process re-energized her own spirit.

Ben called Melissa from the rescue the day she returned from Florida.

"Hello Ben," she chimed. "I have great news, I received over ten applications to adopt Melanie, and I'll start to review them tomorrow."

"I have even better news," he told her. "I'm going to adopt Melanie."

"Ben, you know the rules, fosters cannot adopt," she added.

"Yes, I do, but please let me explain," Ben said, as he went into the story of Lucy's mothering and how Melanie thinks she is her mother. He informed Melissa that Melanie with the wrong family would either bite someone or end up in the pound. Ben pleaded his case bordering on begging. When it came to Lucy, Ben was her over-indulgent owner. He was crazy about his dog, and he loved the idea of her having a companion. Melissa, as are most rescue people, is a compassionate and caring person. She recognized the passion Ben had for his dog and sensed he would be a caring and attentive owner. Melissa made an exception on that day; one Ben is forever grateful for. He filled the adoption application she forwarded to him. It was a twenty-two-page questionnaire of his life. He happily filled it out, signed on the dotted line, paid his adoption fee, and added a generous donation. Melanie was his. She has been a part of Ben's life ever since.

Chapter 3

The traffic started to move as Ben, and the dogs approached the strip malls on the way to the beach. It was the Rehoboth shopping district consisting of sporting outlet stores, Wal-Mart, Kmart, several food stores, and a host of restaurants and specialty shops. The one-lane road opened into three and filtered cars to the several beach areas more efficiently.

Ben was starving after the slow, arduous ride down Route 1. Spotting a deli he knew, Ben pulled into the parking lot and was relieved to have silence from the rush of the air conditioner when he killed the engine. He leashed up his dogs and gathered up the vomit covered towel and threw it into his trunk. He looked forward to a good lunch; the place was a great American-style deli just outside of Dewey Beach with an indoor bar and grill. The deli had ample outdoor patio seating that allowed dogs. Ben picked a table in the shade and with enough room for the dogs. The patio was hot but tolerable. A hot breeze wafted by, carrying the scent of French fries and burgers. Lucy had her nose in the air savoring the smells. She knew lunch was on the way. Ben ordered a cheesesteak with fries for himself and off the children's menu a cheeseburger each for Melanie and Lucy. The waitress arrived with their order and a dog bowl of cold water. He broke up the burgers and placed them on a napkin at the dogs' feet. Lucy daintily gobbled up her burger. Melanie was green, still wobbly and sick from the ride. She stared cross-eyed at her burger. Normally Melanie would wolf down the treat, but the stop and go traffic had stolen her appetite. Lucy eyed Melanie's burger after she finished hers. If Melanie did not eat, Lucy would surely not pass on the opportunity for more burger.

"Oh no, Lucy," Ben said. "We'll take Mel's burger to go, she'll be hungry later."

He packed her lunch in a to-go bag, loaded his dogs back in the car and headed for the condo he rented for the weekend.

Ben had rented a dog-friendly place a half block from the bay, and one and a half blocks to the beach. It had three bedrooms and two baths, one for himself and Sandy. Mel and Lucy each had her own bedroom. It was the one time they were allowed on the bed, and they loved it. Ben was pleased the condo was clean with polished hardwood floors throughout. There was a large deck with glass sliders from the living room and a door from the kitchen.

It was the top unit of a two-story building, and the deck had a beautiful view of the bay. Dewey Beach, Delaware was a small beach town known for its congenial, dog-friendly atmosphere. It was about twenty blocks long and in the center of town only two blocks wide. It had Rehoboth Bay to the west and the wide-open expanse of the Atlantic Ocean to its east. The beach was open to pets before ten in the morning and reopened for pets after five in the evening. During daytime hours it was your typical family beach. The rest of the time it was the world's largest dog park.

Chapter 4

Manuel Garcia and his girlfriend Maria Alvarez had also just arrived at Dewey. Manuel had none of the traffic problems as his forty-six-foot StarCraft motored into the calm waters of the Rehoboth Bay Beach and Yacht Club. Vinny, his cousin and business associate, deftly steered the boat into its mooring. Maria lay on the bow's deck in her pink string bikini, sunning herself. Manuel grabbed a stern line and threw it to a waiting shore hand as the boat glided into the slip. Manuel was met by the club's manager, Joseph DiSalvo. Mr. DiSalvo was thrilled to have his newest member of the club docking for the first time.

"I'm so pleased to meet you, Mr. Garcia," DiSalvo said in a friendly tone. "Is this lovely lady your wife?" as he eyed the shapely Maria.

"Girlfriend. Did my car service get here?" Manuel growled.

"I don't believe your car is here yet. I'll check, sir. Will you be staying on your boat? We have all the available hookups and one of the finest restaurants in Rehoboth," he added.

"We'll be staying in Dewey. Have my boat gassed up, I plan on using it tomorrow," he said as he stepped onto the dock "C'mon, Maria, move it," he said as Mr. DiSalvo helped her step off the boat.

"Which way is the bar?" he asked as he added, "Vinny, don't forget the bags."

"Yes, sir, the lounge is the first building right off the dock," DiSalvo said as he wondered who had recommended this "gentleman." Manuel turned as he walked off the dock with Maria, "Vinny, I'll order you a cold one, make sure you bring the bags." He said, "Let me know as soon as the car service arrives."

"Yes, sir, I will. Enjoy your stay in Rehoboth; feel free to let me know if there's anything I can do to make your stay more pleasant," Mr. Disalvo stated.

Manuel turned and headed in the direction of the bar, ignoring his host.

Manuel and Maria walked into the clubhouse as if they owned the club.

"How many in your party?" the hostess asked.

"Where's the bar, sweets?" Manuel asked in a distracted voice. The hostess raised her hand gesturing to the bar room. "Right over…"

"I got it," Manuel interrupted as he steered Maria to the bar off the main dining room. Maria looked around the opulent dining room with carved oak tables and chairs and ornate crystal chandeliers. She turned to comment to Manuel but thought better of it when she viewed his scowl. The bartender was in an animated conversation with two golfers sitting at the bar.

"Bring two Coronas and a Mojito for the lady to my table, make sure they're ice cold," Manuel barked as he walked by interrupting their conversation. The bartender gave an apologetic shrug to his patrons as he opened two Coronas. The waitress brought their drinks just as Vinny made his way to the table. The trio toasted their new business just as Mr. DiSalvo interrupted to inform them their limo had arrived.

"Your Town Car is just outside of the clubhouse. I asked the driver to wait in the circle."

"Yeah, yeah," Manuel muttered as he took a big swig of his beer. The duo had a significant transaction to attend to the following day. Dewey was a low-key, relaxed town. They felt it would be off the radar of law enforcement. Manuel's recently acquired beachfront condo was the perfect hideaway for some relaxation and anonymity. He had a top-floor unit with a beachfront view. It had four sliders off a large family room to an ordinary, multi-tiered deck that sat just behind the dunes. There were four bedrooms, five baths, and a gourmet kitchen. After the round of drinks at the yacht club, they headed to the Town Car that was waiting to take them to the new condo. Manuel was pleased with his new acquisition; he thought to himself that the condo was a great deal. The trio settled themselves in the condo. Manuel placed the suitcase with the five hundred thousand dollars for the transaction under his bed. He was courting a new supplier who was undercutting the other South American growers his syndicate used. It was a gutsy move on the part of a new grower. The supplier was very paranoid and insisted Manuel make the first transaction himself. The merchandise would be boated up from Miami Beach to him tomorrow. He and Vinny decided they would make a vacation out of it.

Manuel, Vinny, and Maria settled into their lavish condo. They sat counting the week's receipts they collected in New Jersey. It was a good week, one hundred and forty-six thousand dollars. The beach season was good for business with the influx of the Jersey Shore wannabes. The Jersey crowd seemed to breed cocaine and heroin addicts.

"Not bad," Manuel said finishing the count.

"With our new supplier we should clear 200K a week," Vinny said as he scooped up some white powder from a plastic bag with his pocket knife and snorted it.

"Enough of that crap," Manuel said as he grabbed the bag and threw it into a torn gym bag with the money.

"I can handle it, Manuel," Vinny said as he picked up the gym bag.

"Handle it? You're gonna end up a junkie like our clientele if you don't go easy on the stuff," Manuel warned. "Put the bag down and don't touch that stuff for a full day and I'll believe you."

"No problem, I can do without it," he said as he placed the bag on the end table aside from the couch. "I have to go; I'm meeting a waitress in Rehoboth. Frank fixed me up with her. He says she's really hot. I'll catch you later," Vinny added as he headed out the sliders to the deck.

Maria had taken a shower and was getting dressed.

"Manuel, take your shower and get dressed, you are taking me to Que Pasa tonight. I heard they have great Mexican food," Maria said.

"Yeah, yeah, I'm drenched with sweat anyway," Manuel said as he headed to the master bathroom.

Chapter 5

Sandy planned to meet Ben around dinner time at the condo. Ben hoped the traffic was lightening up for her. Sandy often seemed indifferent to his dogs. It was ironic that she was responsible for his adopting Lucy. Sandy never wanted Lucy, she wanted her sister Faith, a beige and white spaniel resembling a Brittany. As it turned out, the rescue brought Lucy, a ratty looking black pup to the home inspection. She was carried into Ben's house and has never left. Sandy seemed to like the dogs, but the more Ben saw of her, the more he suspected she was a latent cat person. She volunteered with several capture and spay programs in Westchester County, New York. Since she had been staying at Ben's house, she had managed to find several stray cats to feed. She had a substantial shaggy pet cat she called Fluffy. Fluffy was a large calico with the disposition of a bobcat. The cat appeared to have a distinct dislike for Ben, and it was mutual. His first encounter with Fluffy was at Sandy's house. She invited him in to wait while she finished her makeup for their date. Fluffy greeted Ben in the magnificent great room of her father's house. He sniffed his boot and proceeded to wrap his claws around Ben's leg and bite through his blue jeans.

"Your cat is biting me," he yelled to Sandy.

"Oh no, she's just playing with you" Sandy giggled to him.

Luckily, he had on thick blue jeans and wore his cowboy boots that night. The damage was only a superficial flesh wound. While her cat was digging into his leg, Sandy went upstairs into the bathroom to finish her face. Ben felt the scraping of Fluffy's teeth against his skin and jerked his leg dislodging the furry beast. They had a five-minute Texas stand-off, Ben stared the feline down, daring it with his eyes to try biting him again. Luckily Fluffy became bored with his adversary and sauntered off. His future encounters were just as awkward. He found himself in a battle of wills with the cat. Fluffy stalked him in Sandy's house. Ben's every movement was measured as Fluffy waited to pounce on his prey. Because of the cat, Ben refused to sleep at Sandy's home. The idea of closing his eyes on this nemesis frightened him. Even making love there, Ben had to make sure Fluffy was locked out of the room, always to the protests of Sandy. He had no desire to have his butt clawed if he became distracted by the passion. Ben used the excuse he was allergic to cats and was grateful her mother became the caretaker of the cat when Sandy moved into his apartment.

Ben carried his bags up to the condo and opened the windows to let the fresh sea air in. A warm ocean breeze brought the scent of saltwater into the room. He went about opening the rooms and let Lucy choose her bed. Lucy was the queen mother of him and Mel. Lucy jumped on the queen-size bed in the spare room and rolled on the cover.

"I guess that one is yours; c'mon, Mel, you have the other room."

Melanie had other designs; she jumped on the bed with Lucy and snuggled up to her. She was still Lucy's baby. Ben threw his bags on the dresser and fetched the sheets he ordered from the laundry service. He proceeded to make the beds and set out water and food for the dogs. It was too bright a day to stay in so he grabbed the leashes saying, "Let's go, girls, the bay is calling."

They headed down the short half block to the bay. The road ended in a small bay beach with a small concrete pad to the left, with benches for sitting. Beyond the bench were bay-front homes with their private docks. The water carved into the shoreline on the right, forming a small lagoon. It was lined with a gazebo, some benches, natural reeds, and a few small trees. A long wooden dock jutted out from a bay hotel complex. A family of four consisting of two small girls and their mother and father sat on its end. The children dipped chicken legs tied to a rope into the water and intently watched for any crabs that might make a meal of the leg. The father, holding a small long-arm net, hovered over the kids ready to snatch up an unsuspecting crab. An empty bucket sat beside the mom; their crabbing skills lacked the quiet and stillness required. It was an idyllic setting for watching sunsets and swimming dogs. Lucy and Melanie bound straight to the water. They waded in up to their chests, searching for seabirds to chase.

They loved the water. Lucy was a champion swimmer; she would fetch a stick or ball until Ben tired from throwing it. Melanie was more of a relaxed swimmer and would paddle casually around looking for birds. Sometimes Mel would fetch a stick back; mostly she would wait in the shallows and steal the prize from other incoming dogs.

It was a beautiful summer afternoon. The sand was hot, and humidity was extremely high for a summer day. There was no breeze on the bay and Ben's shirt was damp from sweat. The dogs looked relaxed and comfortable paddling around the bay. Ben was jealous. Ben found a weather-beaten stick washed up near the patch of reeds nearby. He threw it out repeatedly, watching Lucy fetch it as Melanie waited in the shallow water for her to return with the hope of stealing the prize. Melanie eventually tired of stealing the stick. Lucy, as always, was ready for more. Ben threw the piece of driftwood as far as he could. Lucy headed straight for it. Paddling like an Olympic swimmer, she would close on her target quickly, leaving a small wake behind. Her tail was always straight out, adjusting her course like the rudder of a boat, steering her right or left. Her coat pulsated from her sides with each stroke like the tentacles of a jellyfish. It was a beautiful sight to watch. Ben threw the stick until his arm hurt; Lucy had endless energy. Melanie, bored with the water, lumbered onto the sand. There, as was her habit, she would roll until she was completely covered. She would have sand sticking to every inch of her body. Ben cringed when he thought of the sand in her eyes and mouth. It was an unavoidable consequence of her sand bath. A young boy, after observing her completed work, referred to her as a cinnamon donut. Mel, a true pigpen, was the cinnamon donut dog for sure.

Chapter 6

It was close to 5:00 in the afternoon and Ben decided to walk over to the beach to see if there were other dogs there. They walked the short one and a half blocks from the condo. Halfway there, Ben already heard the muffled roar of the surf as seagulls flew above the dunes with their high-pitched laugh. The road ended at the dunes, which were lined by a cedar and wire fence that protected the delicate grasses and plants that held the dunes together. The dunes are the shore's first line of defense from the pounding surges of storms. A serpentine path cut through the dunes to allow beachgoers access to the roaring surf. Lucy and Mel knew the beach well. He released them from their leash fifty yards from the path through the dunes. They bounded off to the beach. Lucy raced ahead and disappeared over the crest of the walkway onto the beach. Mel, lumbering behind, hit the sand-road interface and stumbled, rolling onto the soft sand. She was such a klutz and was a stark contrast to the agility of Lucy. Ben laughed to himself as she righted herself and headed over the dune.

The beachfront homes have been transformed from modest beach houses and some row condos into lavish million-dollar condos. They are razing the more modest homes in favor of multi-level, multi-decked glass-front condos. The condos blended into a connected series of decks from one block to the next, a private multilevel boardwalk. This is not your typical boardwalk. Instead of shops and games, there is upscale patio furniture and "good people" enjoying their wine and cocktails. On the deck to Ben's right was a rare sight. There was a family with children ranging from about six to fourteen. They were laughing and playing a board game and even took the time to wave as Ben passed. Children were few and far between in the million-dollar homes. Apparently the "good people" did not have the time for families, choosing a beachfront condo in place of college tuition.

Ben walked over the crest of the dune into doggie heaven. The ocean spread endlessly to the horizon, lapping incessantly at the ample beach. The cyclical roar of breaking waves was the timekeeper of the earth. A faint ocean breeze was cooling the hot beach. It carried the hint of the ocean spray and the fresh ocean scents. Lucy, with Melanie in tow, cantered down the beach after a chocolate Lab. The beach still had the late-day stragglers, beachgoers lusting after every minute they spent on the sand. Umbrellas and sand chairs were randomly scattered along the sand with an occasional sleeping sunbather or a family with young children. There were still a few teens daring the surf. The lifeguards' chairs were pulled back to the dunes and their sentinels on the way to dinner, done for the day. Soon the call for supper or the influx of fishermen and dogs would chase the last of the beachgoers home. Ben gazed down the expanse of beach and watched dogs appear as if out of the sand. They ran from between the dunes in their mad dash to the water. Owners with leashes and an armamentarium of dog supplies slowly appeared and followed their faithful beasts. They carried poop bags, water, water dishes, balls, sticks, and a variety of floating toys, brushes, everything and anything they could think their pet would want or need. It was once said if aliens observed this ritual of pampering, picking up behind, and fawning over our dogs, they could only come to the conclusion that the dog was the intelligent one of the group. The dog park was open!

Chapter 7

Ben caught up with his pups just as the owner of a muscular brown Labrador Retriever threw a floating rope toy into the surf. The fearless Lab sprang into the churning surf. Like an ocean otter, he paddled furiously, vaulting himself over the crests of the waves as they broke. Up and over he flew straight to his toy. Melanie tried to follow, and as the Lab vaulted over the cresting wave, the slowly paddling Mel was sucked into the crest. The wave engulfed her. Ben started kicking off his shoes as he ran to the ocean. He had just entered the water as Mel popped out of the raging foam, nose up gasping for air, making a high-pitched seal sound as she coughed. The wave dumped her unceremoniously on the beach and receded with a gurgle of a laugh. Lucy watched from the edge of the water with a disapproving look at the saturated hound. Ben's racing heart slowed, as he pulled Melanie away from the water, relieved she did not drown. The Lab's owner raced to them asking,

"Is your dog alright?"

"I think so," Ben replied as Mel's seal bark quieted, and she found her feet again.

"Your dog isn't a strong swimmer," he added as the Lab returned from the deep, unscathed, dropping his toy at his owner's feet.

"She overestimates her abilities. This isn't the first time she floundered in the surf. You would think she would've learned by now she's not an ocean dog," Ben said.

"You should keep her on a leash, she's going to drown," the Lab's owner said with concern.

"I'm sure after this experience she'll respect the waves and stay at the edge," Ben added.

"Dumb dog, I guess" the Lab's owner added as he threw the toy back in the surf with his faithful Lab bounding through the waves again.

"Yeah, dumb dog," Ben concluded.

The Lab grabbed its toy and turning, rode a wave back to the shore. What a fantastic display of poise and athleticism. Mel was recovering; she switched gears and stayed at the water's edge trying to steal the toy as the other dog returned it. The Lab would have none of it; he spun to avoid Mel as she tried to snatch his toy. They melted into a spinning frenzy of fur. Ben had a great laugh over it, and as they walked to meet the next group of playing hounds, all Ben could think was "dumb dog."

Lucy, on the other hand, was a champion swimmer. She instinctively knew the power of the ocean and her limitations. If Ben asked her to fetch a stick, she would time the waves and set off when she had a clear path past the breakwater. Ben did not tempt her loyalty and feared her being lost due to her slim build and lightweight. Lucy was happy enough watching the Labs and their crazy water adventures and keeping an eye on her baby, Melanie, from the shore. Lucy would watch out for Mel as she played. Mel had no "street" smarts and tried to play with any dog she encountered. She had no judge of temperament, and her overtures of play were often ignored or irritated a disinterested dog. If another dog was too rough or irritable with Melanie, Lucy would insert herself between them and cleave Melanie away from trouble. She was a good mother. If left to her own judgment Mel would be chewed on by Chihuahuas, knocked over by shepherds, and would take, good-naturedly, whatever another dog had to dish out. Yes, a dumb dog. Good thing she had Lucy to look after her.

The two played another half hour with Cockerpoos, Labradoodles, Puggles, Shitpoos, Golden Doodles, and every other breed of designer dog you could think of. Lucy, forever the hunter was often distracted by feeding birds. Lucy would sprint after the small seabirds that raced after the receding waves to eat the delicacies they left behind. The birds would fly the water's edge a short distance and taunt their pursuer to enter the surf as they circled around to their meal. Lucy was wise to their game. She had no desire to be drowned by a bird's folly and would circle back herself, frustrating the bird-brains. Mel soon tired. She went into cinnamon donut mode rolling in the sand, covered from head to toe with the beautiful granular stuff. Lucy was ready too. Mel was too traumatized for Ben to get her into the ocean to clean up. He decided he would give them a hose bath at the condo and get them ready for bed. Sandy would be getting in soon; he thought he would have her pick up dinner on the way in and have a nice quiet supper at the condo. He was tired himself from the day's activity.

On the walk back with the dogs, Ben called Sandy on her cell phone; "Hey babe, how are you?"

"I'm in Dover. I should be there in about an hour, the traffic is just starting to move," she said.

"I'll call an order into the Captain's Table, if you can pick it up on the way in. What you are in the mood for?"

Sandy wanted to go out to eat at Que Pasa on the bay. Ben tried to convince her to pick up their dinner so they could have a nice romantic meal on the condo's deck. She was intent on eating out and ignored Ben. She insisted on Que Pasa and warned he had better be ready when she arrived. Sandy would be in by seven, which gave him enough time to clean the dogs and shower and shave. Que Pasa's cuisine was Mexican with a southwest flare. They were famous for their Wednesday night taco toss. The beer was cold, and the Mojitos and daiquiris flowed like water. Que Pasa had a relaxed atmosphere with tables on a bay beach as well as an indoor dining room. They had a rectangular bar next to their beach seating. It would open on all four sides with the raising of great garage door walls exposing a four-sided bar with all the amenities one would expect. Ben liked Que Pasa because they allowed dogs at the beach tables. He brought them there often for lunch when he could enjoy a chicken quesadilla and a cold beer and watch his girls chase seabirds and paddle around the bay.

"Alright, Que Pasa it is, see you soon," Ben said as he hung up.

"Let's clean you two up, we have a dinner engagement," he told Mel and Lucy.

Ben gave his dogs a hose bath; Lucy loved the bathing; it was an extension of a good scratching. When Ben would work in the shampoo, she leaned in with a look of utter contentment on her. Mel, on the other hand, disliked bathing. It was perplexing to Ben that a dog who would not hesitate to jump into the ocean would have such an aversion to a bath. He battled Mel through her bath holding her firmly to prevent her from bolting away. Ben scrubbed sand out of every inch of her skin as she fought and shook, completely saturating Ben. She had sand in every fold and crevice. It was amazing how much sand would wash out of her hair.

"Well girl, if you don't like baths then you need to drop the cinnamon donut roll," he told Mel as she squirmed. He had to keep Mel leashed after a bath, or she would just find something else to roll in. He towel-dried his mutts and headed up the condo stairs to shower and dress for dinner.

Chapter 8

Ben had just finished dressing when he heard Sandy's car pull in. She walked in the door with a "hello" as Mel and Lucy ran to greet her. She wore a pink sundress with yellow sunflowers and a matching pink sun hat with blond curls spilling out the sides. She had a matching pink purse and pink clogs.

"Oh my God, you have the dogs getting everything wet," she complained as she dragged Mel out on the deck. Lucy followed obediently behind. Sandy locked them on the deck as Ben sauntered out of the bedroom clean and ready for dinner.

"Hey babe, good timing, we're starving," he said as he opened the slider to the deck. Lucy and Mel rushed back into the condo. Ben laughed to himself at the sight of Sandy as images of the pink panther strikes again flashed in his head.

"We? You're not taking the dogs to dinner?" she said in an unhappy tone.

"Of course they're coming; they're clean and hungry and look quite ready to go," he said.

"They're damp, and the restaurant will make us sit on the beach," she quipped.

"It's a beautiful night, and it will be a spectacular sunset so quit griping and let's eat," he chimed back. Sandy knew she had no choice but to agree. Ben was utterly obsessed with his dogs.

They leashed the dogs and walked the three blocks to Que Pasa. The restaurant was in the center of town. There is a ring of six restaurants with the block ending at a bay beach with an extensive volleyball court in the center of the road's end. The Lighthouse was Ben's favorite place to eat. It had a large wraparound deck over the water. The restaurant boasted an American light fare and spectacular sunset views. Most of all they allowed the dogs to dine on the deck. On the other side of the volleyball court was the Rusty Rudder, a family restaurant with a bayside bar featuring a calypso band nightly. They did not allow dogs, but you could enjoy the music from the deck of the Lighthouse. The Rudder has a long public dock. Locals would tie their boats up and enjoy the food and cocktails and ferry themselves back home when done. Some would just anchor their boat in the small cove by the volleyball court and sit enjoying their fare from home and listen to the bands playing. Children and adults would fish and crab off the dock. There was an Irish pub with typical pub food, Halloran's, on the right-hand corner of the main road with a small patio that allowed dogs and on the other side of the main street was a Hawaiian theme restaurant, Maui Maui, with creative island theme fare. Ben's restaurant criteria included pet-friendly dining, to the dismay of Sandy.

Chapter 9

Sandy was Ben's latest fling. She was a cute, petite woman a couple of years younger than Ben. She had a peculiar personality. She was what some would describe as "prissy" and had a conflicted sense of cleanliness. Anything the dogs touched was dirty, but a cat walking across the dinner table is beautiful. She was the essence of a dysfunctional relationship. She was a person who could be caring one minute and selfish the next. She just had no consistency in her commitment to a relationship. She could be one of the most selfish people Ben knew. He attributed her spoiled personality as the direct result of being brought up in a family of boys. They must have treated her like a princess when she was younger. Sandy liked being the center of attention. Ben believed she was openly jealous of the attention he paid to his two dogs. Ben often found himself comparing his people relationships to his dog relationships. Sadly, his dog relationships were winning. Ben was convinced Lucy was a person reincarnated. He would watch her reactions to his personal and emotional situations and think she comprehended them. Lucy would yawn, roll her eyes, or just give him her penetrating stare that he would interpret as cognition. Ben believed Lucy was a creature of gestures unable to produce words and join in the conversation, but her gestures often spoke louder than words. She was his Enzo; behind those deep brown eyes laid a cognitive understanding mind. Melanie, on the other hand, had a nerdy, naïve personality. Ben found her hard to read; he believed her persona lay deeper, hidden by layers of dog. When it came to Melanie, Ben kept looking for her inner persona. Someday she may show her hidden person; perhaps she was just a dog. Either way, he loved her.

Ben, Sandy, and the dogs were seated at a table on the bay beach. It was a comfortable night, and the sun was just starting to set. Hues of red and orange were streaked across the horizon dotted with silvery puffs of clouds. The picture was completed by a sizeable orange-yellow sun slowly sliding into the bay. The water shimmered with a spectrum of color. The picture was disturbed only by the occasional passing boat, ferrying diners or partygoers to their destinations. The waitress took their food and drink orders. Ben ordered off the children's menu for the dogs; cheeseburgers for his girls. Lucy tucked herself under Ben's chair as Melanie went into her cinnamon donut routine.

"Oh God, there she goes again. Why can't she be more like Lucy?" Sandy complained.

"No can do, Mel has to be Mel, my big pig pen," Ben said chuckling as the waitress brought the food. She also supplied a bucket of ice water for the dogs.

"I thought they may like some cold water, your dogs are soo cute," the waitress commented.

At that moment Melanie shook, peppering them and the adjoining tables with a spray of sand. The table on their right laughed at Melanie as Ben apologized. The table to their left looked annoyed. The waitress laughed, commenting, "Dogs will be dogs."

Sandy protested, "Why do we have to bring these animals everywhere we go? You don't see me dragging Fluffy around."

Ben's mind flashed "Thank God, no devil cat tonight."

Mel was oblivious to the mess and dug into the burger Ben placed on a napkin in front of her. Lucy delicately ate her burger as Mel wolfed hers down and then proceeded to eat the napkin. The dog could eat!

Ben overheard the gentleman from the table on the left tell the woman he was with, "Just keep your mouth shut; I don't want a scene here over a dog."

"There's sand in my food," she said annoyed.

"We need to keep a low profile here, I'll order you another dish," he replied.

"I'm so sorry," Ben told the couple, "please let me pay for your meal," he added.

The man in his mid-fifties was oddly dressed wearing a light jacket over a polo shirt. It was way too hot for a jacket in a very casual restaurant. He wore socks and what looked to be wing tips, another strange choice in a sea of flip flops, sandals, and sockless topsiders.

"No need," he said, "stuff happens," he added in a rough voice as he turned back to the woman. Manuel Garcia was already unhappy. His girlfriend Maria insisted they sit on the bay beach to eat. She loved the romantic setting. He hated sitting on the beach with its lack of air conditioning. He needed the cooling. It was his trademark to always wear his coat in public. He carried a custom-made, snub nose revolver in a special pocket his tailor added to the coat. In his line of work, you could never be too careful; he would not be caught off guard without his gun. The sweat was rolling down his back and sand was in his shoes. He was in the mood to punch out the dog guy. He thought it was lucky for the dog guy he had a big transaction going down tomorrow and didn't need to attract any attention. He watched as the big dog settled down and fell asleep in the sand. "Lucky for its owner," Manuel thought.

Chapter 10

Ben and Sandy ate as the sun went down. Mel lay in the sand fast asleep. There was only quiet chatter from the surrounding tables, and they had no further incidents at the restaurant. They enjoyed a relaxing after-dinner cocktail as the sun had sunk into the bay and the moon was rose over the bar's roof. Ben suggested they go for a walk. He paid the check and leashed his sleepy dogs. The couple strolled down the block to the beach side. Lucy and Melanie, realizing where they were going, we're excited to be back at the beach. Ben let them loose, and they tore through the dune path to the beach. At the sand's edge, the couple shed their shoes. With shoes in hand, Sandy and Ben leisurely strolled along the beach, walking around fishermen's lines and watching kids running with glow sticks and flashlights. Lucy and Mel ran in the darkness. They would occasionally catch a glimpse of the dogs moving across the sand or hear the telltale tinkle of their tags. Lucy knew the block home and headed for the dune path back to the street with Mel following. Lucy was ready for bed. They lost sight of the dogs but knew they would wait at the end of the path. Ben was in no rush to leave the beach. It was a beautiful clear night with a pleasant breeze. The fishing boats twinkled on the black ocean as the stars twinkled in the sky. Both sky and ocean left him in awe of their vastness. He breathed the sea air in deeply, dreaming of someday owning a beach house. He watched a shooting star streak across the sky and thought, "It doesn't get any better than this."

Sandy and Ben walked to Lucy sitting at the start of the road, illuminated by the streetlight. The condos on the beach displayed their extravagant decor with lamplight spilling out of their curtainless glass sliders. Deck lights spotted the maze of interconnecting decks with surprisingly few people. The children he saw earlier on the south side of the street gave themselves away with spurts of giggles and aimless chatter. Mel was nowhere to be seen.

"Where did she go now? MEL, MEL," Ben shouted

"Maybe she got lost, not that it would be a bad thing," Sandy said.

"Don't even joke; Mel's my baby," he said as he continued to call, "MEL, MEL, HERE GIRL."

Mel was prone to wandering, never far, but she would eventually bound back when she was ready.

"MEL! COME, MEL" he shouted.

Mel, on cue, appeared on the north side of the street at the top of a stair leading to the upper inter-weaved decks of the condos. She had a large bag or sack in her mouth. It was the prize which had called her away; his dumb dog was always playing with a stick or trash she found.

"Come here, girl, let's go," Ben said to her.

She started down the stairs, catching her paw in the strap of the bag she had found. Mel tumbling down the stairs with the bag following.

"Oh my," Sandy said, startled

Ben walked to Mel. "Are you alright, you klutz?" he asked Melanie. She rolled back on all fours and grabbed the bag again in her mouth. It was some sort of a canvas gym bag. Mel held it proudly. It was tattered and what appeared to be a dollar bill was hanging out of a tear. Ben grabbed the bag. "Drop it" he commanded. Mel let go, and he inspected her find. Ben pulled at the bill and realized it was a hundred dollar bill and it looked real.

"What is it?" Sandy asked.

"It's a hundred-dollar bill" Ben replied as he opened the bag.

"Is it play money?" Sandy asked.

"No, it looks real, and the bag is full of more bills," he said as he sorted through it. "If these are real, there are thousands here."

"Real money? We have to find who she has taken it from," Sandy said with concern.

Ben pulled out a large bag of a white powder.

"This doesn't look so good; I think it's drugs. The money must be drug money."

"Oh my," Sandy exclaimed. "We'd better get it to the police."

"Come on, let's go, standing under this light holding a bag of drugs and money may not be smart. Let's walk over to the police station," Ben said.

They leashed the dogs and headed to the police station. Dewey was a small town, maybe twenty blocks total. The police station was just off the center of town. Ben walked with Melanie's find tucked under his arm. He looked around as he walked, fearful the owner of the bag would be after them. Only a few distracted teens and some couples enjoying the night were seen. Traffic was brisk through town as they crossed the main and only road. The weekend crowd was in. They walked nervously to the station; the building was dark, only the front path lights were lit. There were no signs of activity in the building, and the door rattled as Ben gave it a tug, the deadbolt unyielding and uninviting. Ben stood staring at the locked door; holding the bag of drugs and money. A nervous sweat rolled down his back as a feeling of dread washed over him.

"Closed," Ben said.

"Closed?" Sandy parroted, "the police close at night?"

"I guess," he answered. "I don't like this at all."

"We'd better get off the street with this," Sandy said.

"You don't have to tell me twice, let's go."

They headed back to the condo walking in silence, each contemplating their next move. They entered the condo and threw the bag on the table. Sandy and Ben stared blankly at the bag for several moments.

"We'd better call the police," Sandy suggested

"I'm not sure that's a good idea. What if the drug dealers have a scanner? It only makes sense they may monitor the police; they'll hear the call and know where and who we are," Ben said.

"Perhaps you're right," she added.

"First thing in the morning we can bring it over to the police station," he said.

"I'll feel much better when that bag is out of this house," Sandy said.

"So will I," Ben added

Ben gave the dogs some water and put them on their beds. They looked tired; he was sure they would sleep all night. Sandy went in to take a shower before bed. Ben sat at the table and stared at the bag of cash and drugs. He started counting the bills and organizing them into piles. Sandy came out wrapped in a towel as he sat counting the cash.

"What are you doing?" she asked in an astonished tone.

"Counting the money. There are over one hundred and forty thousand dollars, all in hundreds," Ben informed her.

"Are you nuts? You're getting your fingerprints all over the money! Besides, it's dirty money," she said.

"I know it's drug money. I was just curious," Ben said.

"No, I meant dirt dirty; you better take a shower if you are going to get in bed with me," Sandy said defiantly.

"Okay, a shower it is," he said eagerly. Ben took it as an invitation.

He stuffed the bills back in the bag and put the bag in the back of the kitchen closet, covering it with vacuum cleaner bags. Ben jumped in the shower and rushed to the bedroom, anticipating what would come next. Sandy was motionless on her side taking muffled rhythmic breaths. "Asleep, oh well," he thought as he climbed into bed and went to sleep himself.

Chapter 11

Manuel enjoyed the evening once the sand dog left. Maria was getting loaded on the Margaritas and was playing footsie with him under the table. She was ripe for the picking, and he was feeling no pain from the tequila shots and beer. The couple headed back to their condo. It was a brand new four-bedroom with a direct view of the ocean. Manuel had picked it up for a bargain. The contractor's son had a big coke habit and was into him for thirty grand. His penchant for fast cars, loose women, and cocaine put him seriously behind on his payments to Manuel. He had a good dad; Manuel paid him six hundred grand cash and a live son for a one million-dollar condo. Manuel felt sorry for the father; he was a good, honest man with a useless son. Manuel knew it would only be a matter of time before the fool for a father will have to bail his son out again. Manuel knew he would be better off disowning his son. He pondered whether he would be doing the father a favor by eliminating the son.

Manuel Garcia was a Cuban born refugee. He came to the United States as one of the boat people when Fidel Castro emptied his jails and sent them in a flotilla to the United States. In Cuba he was a petty criminal, dabbling in stolen goods and dealing cocaine. Once he hit the gold-paved streets of Miami, he organized a drug ring with a group of Colombians he met during a short stint in a United States jail. He grew his enterprise and moved into the lucrative New York, East Coast drug trade. His ruthless practices moved his cartel to the top of the drug trade. With his right-hand man and cousin Vinny Zambia, he controlled a large part of the East Coast's trade within ten years.

Manuel entered the condo from the street side, and he immediately noticed the glass sliders to the deck were open.

"Maria, you left the sliders open again," Manuel scolded her.

"I was sure I had closed them before we left," she said as she peeled off her damp blouse and skirt. "Come on, Manny, don't ruin the mood, and come to bed. You're too paranoid," she said as he noticed the bag his partner Vinny had left was no longer on the end table. It was a bag with their week's proceeds and Vinnie's personal stash.

"Did you move Vinny's bag?" he asked.

"I didn't move anything, Manny" she replied. "Are you coming to bed or what?"

"We have a problem, then. Vinny left our money right here next to the slider, and it's gone," Manuel added in an annoyed tone.

"Gone, who would take it?" Marie said

"It was right here when we left, and you left the door open asking someone to come and get it."

"It has got to be here, nobody would dare steal from you."

"You better start tearing this place apart and pray someone didn't take my money," he threatened.

Maria felt a sense of panic as she started looking through the condo. Manuel called Vinny. His cell phone rang twice before he picked up.

"What's up, Manny?"

"Vinny, did you come back to the condo and take the bag of money?"

"No, why are you asking me that?" Vinny asked.

"I bet those kids did it, they're always playing on the decks," Maria said, trying to soothe his growing dark mood.

"We have a problem; the bag is missing. I was hoping you came back for your stash. Maria left the sliders open. Someone must have snatched the bag; she thinks it might be those kids who are always around," he informed Vinny.

"How could you let something like this happen, Manny? My coke was in the bag," he added.

"Screw your coke, my money is gone," Manuel barked at the phone.

"Calm down," he assured Manny "I'm on my way, check the condo just in case, we will get whoever took it."

"Maria is checking the condo now. I'll look around outside; get here fast," he said.

Manuel checked the attached decks and looked for any clue where the bag may have gone. "That stupid broad cost me big time. Someone's going to pay for my bag," he mumbled under his breath.

Chapter 12

Ben was restless; his mind kept wandering to the bag in the closet. He finally dozed off to a troubled sleep. He was chased through the streets of Dewey by a madman. His pursuer closed the distance to him. Ben tried to run faster, but his dog leashes were dragging behind him, holding him back as he tried to run. He made it to the bay, and he and the dogs ran into the water. The water was strange and thick, and he waded into it. He looked back for his dogs and realized that the water was blood. He had a vision of his dogs lying in a pool of blood and woke startled and drenched with sweat. Sleep was elusive as the vision of the dogs in blood remained on his mind. Ben tossed and turned but could not shake the vision. He watched the sunrise through the bedroom window, exhausted but relieved the night had passed. Lucy and Mel were up at dawn ready for their walk. Lucy jumped up and snuggled next to Ben. She tucked her body against his and licked his hand. She pressed against him and let out a small yawn. Ben wished the lightly snoring Sandy was half as affectionate with him as Lucy.

Mel stared at him from the bedside with her "What, me worry?" look. Ben wondered how his dumb dog was able to get them into this mess. Sandy lay next to him in a tangle of sheets. He shook her until she stirred.

"Get dressed, I want to get that bag out of the house and to the police as fast as possible," he commanded.

"Go without me. I'm tired," Sandy replied sleepily as she peered up through half-closed eyes with the sheet creases still on her face.

"No way, babe, I'm not walking into the police station with a bag full of money and drugs and some crazy story about my dog taking it from someone's condo without a witness," Ben said emphatically, "so get your pretty little butt out of bed," he added as he proceeded to spank her.

"Alright, alright, I'm up," she said.

They both dressed in shorts and light shirts. The temperature was already pushing eighty. It was going to be a hot day. Sandy had a quick breakfast of yogurt and toast. Ben couldn't eat; his stomach was in knots. He retrieved the bag from the closet and placed it in a black kitchen garbage bag. Not too conspicuous, he thought, everyone, walks around town with their garbage. Lucy and Melanie waited patiently, staring at the door with tails wagging.

They leashed the dogs and headed with the black garbage bag in hand to the police station. It was a beautiful summer morning. A cool breeze blew off the bay with the smell of saltwater. It was already hot but still comfortable. Ben was anxious to get rid of the package. He wondered how long he would be at the station explaining away the bag of drugs. Ben had an uneasy feeling in his stomach, perhaps it was just hunger. They walked briskly in silence, only stopping to let Mel and Lucy take care of business. The police station had a conspicuous absence of police cars or activity. They walked up to the door and as Ben tugged there was the distinctive clank of the deadbolt. He stood staring unbelievingly that the door was still locked tight. His nerves returned as the sweat started to drip down his back again and he wiped an arm over his damp head. Thoughts of trouble swam in his head.

"What the…. it's locked!" he protested.

Sandy was reading a notice on the adjacent door.

"Look at this," she said.

Ben read the notice: "Closed for the weekend. IF THIS IS AN EMERGENCY, CALL 911. Other police business can be conducted at the Dover police station, 211 West Avenue, Dover."

"Is this for real? How can they close a police station?" he said, annoyed

"Maybe we should call 911," Sandy said.

"Yeah, and we can just wait here for the drug dealers to show up to a closed police station. This is crazy. There's no way I'm going to drive a half hour to Dover on a Saturday morning. With beach traffic it will be a five-hour excursion," he said.

"What do you expect us to do with the bag of money and drugs?" Sandy asked.

"I'll just put it back in the closet until Monday, and tonight we're going to have a really nice dinner on the crooks who put us in a mess," he added.

"Are you crazy? We're not going to spend a dime of drug money. I want that bag gone," she said in a half-frightened, half-irritated tone.

"It's back to the closet for now; I need to think," Ben said.

Chapter 13

Manuel and Vinny had no luck finding the bag. They scoured the condo through the night. Manuel was in a rage as he and Vinny overturned every piece of furniture in the condo. Maria locked herself in the bathroom, fearing his rage would turn to her. Morning came with no sign of the bag, Manuel sent Vinny out to check the locals to see if they had any word of the bag or someone who became a big spender overnight. He was checking all the decks again when he spotted those kids coming down to play in the street. He called them over and questioned them about playing on the decks and the bag. The little one asked if it was the doggie's bag.

"What dog's bag? Was it a blue gym bag?" he asked them.

They told him they saw a beige dog with the bag last night. It came from his condo's side of the decks. "Just my luck to have a dog wander into my condo and take the bag of money," he thought. He questioned them about the dogs. The children didn't know where the dog lived. The older child of the group told Manuel the dog was with a man and woman and a smaller black dog. He had the children describe the couple. He was given a generic description of an older man with black hair and a pretty woman with blond hair. Manuel was frustrated at how little the kids noticed about the couple, but they could describe the dogs in detail, even to the color of the dog collar and tags they wore. The kids saw the couple walking the dogs on the beach. Manuel assumed they must be staying nearby since they use the beach access on this block.

Chapter 14

Sandy and Ben walked in silence back to the condo. "Wait here with the dogs, I'm going to put the bag back, and we'll get some coffee and let the dogs run on the beach a little." Ben put the bag back into the pantry closet and recovered it with the vacuum bags. He returned to Sandy and the dogs, and they walked to a small country store on the main road. It was a mom and pop convenience store with great fresh brewed coffee. Ben bought coffee and Danish for Sandy and himself and a buttered croissant for Lucy and Melanie. They sat on the wooden bench in front of the store. Sandy fed the dogs their croissant as she sipped her coffee.

"I'm going to call the chief. I'll bet he'll be able to help us," Ben told Sandy.

Ben counted Chief Abraham of his hometown Montvale as a friend. He dialed the chief and his secretary Marla answered.

"Hello, Montvale police, can I help you?"

"Marla, it's Ben Grece, can I speak with the chief, please? Tell him it's an urgent matter," he said.

"Oh hi, Ben, the chief is getting a physical exam this morning. I expect him back around noon," Marla said.

"Can you ask him to call me as soon as he gets in?" he added.

"I'll let him know the first thing, Ben," she said.

"Thanks, Marla. It's imperative," he said, emphasizing the point as he hung up.

"Damn the chief is unavailable," he said.

"The more I think about this, I think we should just leave the bag at the police station and let them find it. We need to wash our hands of this. I don't want our names involved in this. I don't want drug dealers looking for revenge because Melanie took their bag. The whole situation is crazy," Ben said.

"The sooner we get rid of the bag the better, if you ask me," Sandy added.

They finished the coffee, and the dogs gobbled down the remainder of their croissant. The couple decided to let the dogs run for a short stint on the beach and then retrieve the bag from the condo and leave the money at the police station by lunchtime. They would let the next finder of the money worry about it. Ben and Sandy walked down the beach block and were at the beginning of the dune where the fateful stairway to cash was. Ben kept Melanie on the leash this time; he did not want her wandering back to the unit where she stole the bag. Ben was slipping off his sneakers when a voice called from behind, "Hey mister, is your dog-friendly?"

"Yes, very friendly," he replied.

"Mind if we pet him?" the boy asked

"She, they're both girls," he told them, "and they love to be scratched."

It was the kids he had seen the day before playing on the deck on the south side of the street. There was an older boy about thirteen, another boy around eleven, and two girls – one eight the other around six. The boys were bare-chested with colorfully patterned board shorts, the girls in adorable flowered bikinis and all of them barefoot. They crowded up to Melanie and Lucy and took turns scratching their ears and petting them.

"This one is funny," the eight-year-old girl said. "She fell down the steps last night."

"You saw her last night?" Sandy asked looking startled.

"Yeah, she fell over the bag she was carrying, it was so funny," the six-year-old added.

Sandy and Ben both had the "oh crap" look on their faces. They had a simultaneous thought, "Who else saw Melanie and the bag?"

"Did anyone else see Melanie fall?" Ben asked.

"I don't know," the oldest boy answered. "A man did ask us this morning if we were playing on the decks last night."

"I told him about your dog playing on the deck," the eight-year-old said.

"He was a mean man," the six-year-old stated, holding her nose.

"He asked about a bag. I asked him if it was the dog's bag. He wanted to know if we knew where your dog lived. I told him we didn't know. We only saw the dogs on the beach," the older girl explained.

"What did the man look like?" Sandy asked.

"He's older…" the older boy said as the youngest girl interrupted "and mean," she said.

"She means he was not very nice, he kept calling us 'you kids' and pointed at us a lot. He had a scary voice," he said.

"And he's cold a lot," the little one said.

"Cold?" Ben repeated.

"He wears a jacket all the time," the elder boy said.

"Yeah, even on the beach," the older girl said.

Ben became nervous as they spoke; this was not a healthy development. The dogs were pulling to go to the beach.

"We have to go," Ben said.

"Goodbye," Sandy added.

"Bye," they said in a chorus.

"Please don't tell the mean man you saw us?" Sandy asked.

"We won't," said the little one.

Ben started walking to the dune path when Sandy interrupted. "Don't you think we should get away from here?"

"We'll let the dogs get a run. We can walk down the beach and take the side roads home," Ben said.

Ben let the dogs loose where they ran straight for the water. The brown Lab was there fetching his toy out of the surf. Melanie arrived at the water's edge just as his owner threw the toy. The Lab bounded over a cresting wave and motorboated toward the toy. Mel, without hesitation, jumped straight into the cresting wave and disappeared into the foam. Ben ran in after her, as Melanie popped up out of the maelstrom a second more massive wave crested over her. The wave hit Ben like a truck, knocking him off his feet. He went under for a second, and as he came up, Melanie popped up coughing like a seal again, swimming furiously. The undertow grabbed her, and she was pulled into the breaking crest of the next wave, her swimming had no effect on her movement. Ben jumped into the foam and felt the submerged dog knocking against his knees. He grabbed her with both hands as she continued to flail in the surf and lifted her over his head with every ounce of strength he had. Ben struggled like a drunken sailor toward the beach, with Melanie in his hands, just as the Lab returned unscathed with his toy. Ben was coughing and heaving for breath as Melanie coughed like a seal and gagged. The Lab's owner just looked at him with a frown and repeated his words from the day before, "Dumb dog," as he walked away. Ben repeated to himself, "Yup, dumb dog." Lucy ran to lick and comfort Mel. Sandy just stared at him.

"I've had enough of the beach, let's go, Ahab," Sandy chided Ben.

Ben had no will to disagree. "Let's go," he added.

Chapter 15

Vinny had returned to the condo, having had no luck, and no information about the money.

"I offered a reward to our contacts for information about the bag," Vinny said.

"It won't be necessary; those kids saw a dog take the bag last night."

"A dog?" Vinny said, unbelieving.

"Yeah, just our crap luck, a dog. Maria left the sliding door open, and some stupid mutt wanders in and takes our money. The dog belongs to a couple who walk their dogs down our block. They must be staying nearby. Grab the binoculars; we're looking for a couple with a beige dog and a black dog. He has black hair, and the woman is blond. They've been walking the dogs on the beach in the mornings and early evening. You take the south side, I'll take the north. I want our money back."

They watched the beach traffic for an hour. Manuel never imagined there would be so many dogs walking on the beach. They had several false alarms; every dog on the beach was either beige or black and with a couple. Most of the women had blond hair. Vinny spotted a couple with the right color dogs.

"Manuel, over here, they're heading to the road a few blocks away," he exclaimed. Sandy called the dogs, leashed them, and headed up the beach to a dune path where they could exit away from the inquiring owner of the bag.

The drug dealers saw the couple with two leashed dogs, one beige one black, heading towards another dune path down the beach. "It looks like it may be them; c'mon let's get them," Manuel said.

Manuel and Vinnie hustled from the deck and through the dune down to the beach towards the couple they had spotted. Sandy and Ben were just about to get off the beach when Ben noticed two men entering hurriedly from the dune path off their street. One wore a t-shirt, and the other wore a jacket, a jacket in eighty-degree weather. All he could think of was the mean man, the drug dealers, the owners of the bag. Ben didn't know if the men saw them or perhaps the children told them they were on the beach. He had no desire to find out.

"Move, Sandy, before we have company," Ben said hurriedly.

"Company? What are you talking about?" she answered.

"I think the bag man is on the beach. Follow me," he said.

"Oh, God. I told you we should have left," she said nervously.

"It must be them because they're running. Vinny, follow them, I'll double back to the main road and see where they go," Manuel said.

They ran through the dune path several blocks from the men. Ben led Sandy and the dogs through the parking lot of a condo complex to an ally easement between a small hotel and behind some homes. When they reached the main street, Ben looked down Route 1; there was no activity on their block.

"Move quickly," he told Sandy.

She obeyed and followed as they hurriedly crossed the road. Manuel ran to the main road and watched to see where they crossed. In a town two to three blocks wide and only one main road, sooner or later they had to cross the street. He crouched behind a small pine tree and sure enough, the two crossed several blocks up the road between a house and a condo complex. Manuel kept them in sight as they made their way along the yards and driveways near the bay.

Ben and Sandy hurried through another condo's parking lot down to the marina. The couple ran along the bay through the yards and condo parking lots to the back entrance of their condo from the adjoining street. Vinny followed behind them. Manuel caught up with Vinny and showed him where they disappeared into the rear entrance of a condo. They headed down the block to the condo.

Chapter 16

Inside, Ben felt safer. Sandy was hysterical.

"I have to get out of here. I can't take this: we could be killed over that bag."

"Calm down," Ben said, as the dogs started barking at a dog walker outside.

"Shut them up, they're looking for your dogs," Sandy screamed.

"Alright," he said as he called the dogs to the back bedroom. Stay put you two," Ben said as he closed the door.

Sandy rushed into the bedroom hurriedly stuffing her clothes into her bag.

"Going somewhere?" Ben said jokingly.

"Anywhere but here. I'm going home; I've had enough of this crap. I hope you and the bag have a great time together," Sandy screeched as she stormed past him to the door.

"C'mon babe, stay, we'll be fine," Ben assured her.

"Goodbye, Ben," she said as the door slammed behind her. He heard the car start and peel off the gravel car port.

Manuel and Vinny saw the woman run out of the condo with a suitcase in hand. She practically vaulted the stairs and jumped hurriedly into her car.

"I'll get her," Vinny reassured Manuel.

"No, let her go, she's running. We need the guy with the bag. I'll go in. I have my piece, stay on the deck and keep an eye out," he said

Her car with tires squealing turned the corner and disappeared out of sight.

Ben found himself alone in the condo. He went into the bedroom and changed into a dry set of clothes, placing his wet wallet and keys on the dresser to dry.

"Alone again. Oh well, at least I have the dogs," Ben said as he walked down the hall to let the dogs out of the bedroom. Ben stopped to go to the bathroom. He heard the front door open, and he walked out of the bathroom saying, "Sandy, I knew you would come back," as he went into the living room. There stood the gentleman from Que Pasa whom Mel had shaken the sand on. He was wearing the jacket over the t-shirt he had on the other night. In his right hand was a small snub-nosed revolver. Ben pondered, "How crazy is this? The guy from the restaurant was the bag man?" He tried to relieve the tension with some humor. "No need for a gun, I told you I'd pay for your meal," Ben said as a look of recognition came over Manuel's face.

"Unbelievable. It was the sand-covered mutt at the restaurant who took my bag?" Manuel said.

"Bag, what bag?" Ben said in a questioning tone.

"Don't play stupid with me. We saw you and the girl with the dogs, and those kids saw your dog take my bag," Manuel said, raising his voice.

"What dogs?" Ben said just as they started to bark at the bedroom door.

"Those dogs," he said, "and we can do this easy or hard, it's your choice. I want the bag, and for your sake, I hope you still have it."

"This is all one big misunderstanding. Mel thought it was a toy. I didn't know who it belonged to," Ben said babbling.

"I hope nothing is missing from it," Manuel threatened.

"I never even opened it. I was asking who owned it around town and I didn't even report it to the police," he added in a trembling voice. Ben's mouth became cottony, and he started sweating profusely.

"I'm sure you never opened it. Do I look like an idiot to you?" Manuel yelled.

"No, sir, I was just saying I…."

"Shut up," Manuel commanded, "I have to figure out what to do with you now."

The last statement did not sound right to Ben. He pictured himself being thrown to the sharks or floating face down in a back bay. "I'll show you the bag is fine and unopened, it's right here," he gestured to the closet.

"Get it slowly," Manuel commanded again.

Ben opened the closet door and moved the vacuum bags producing the torn gym bag.

"See, just like we found it," he smiled.

"Hand it over," Manuel said with his free hand outstretched.

The dogs were barking crazily from the bedroom, scratching at the door. Just as Ben was handing the bag to his armed visitor, the dogs had scratched the bedroom door open. They charged down the hall with Melanie in front. Melanie saw the visitor directly in front of her and tried to stop her charge. The floor was well waxed and Mel, a sliding ball of fur, slammed into the legs of Ben's captor before he had time to react. His feet were swept out from under him, and he banged hard onto the hardwood floor. Ben pulled the bag from his grip and without hesitation ran out the front door calling to his girls.

"Melanie, Lucy, come." They followed obediently on Ben's heels. The younger man, Vinny, was standing at the top of the stairs on the porch. Ben surmised he was the apparent lookout. As he turned toward the commotion, Ben lowered his shoulder and hit him, linebacker style. He tumbled down the stairs ahead of Ben with a grunt. Ben jumped over him as he hit the lower landing with Melanie and Lucy using his belly as a springboard, bouncing on the thug and following Ben down the stairs.

Chapter 17

Lucy, Melanie, and Ben, free of confinement, hastily ran down the block. Ben was clutching the cursed bag. Lucy sprinted past Ben; it was great fun to her as she headed to the bay. Melanie passed, grabbed the bag and accelerated after Lucy. Ben, already winded, was barely able to yell, "No, bad dog, Melanie, give me the bag." Melanie just continued after Lucy.

Manuel's chest hurt as he picked himself up from the floor. He had fallen on his gun, driving it into his ribcage. He ran out the door in pursuit of his money. Cursing under his breath, he saw Vinny pulling himself up on the lower landing. Vinny apparently suffered the same fate.

Manuel muttered, "That dumb dog."

From behind him, Ben heard, "Hey, come back here," as he turned to see the two drug dealers scrambling off the porch. Ben turned left along the water's edge, calling the dogs to him. He chose to run along the backyards and docks of the bay-front homes, hoping the obstacles of fencing and docks would slow his pursuers. The trio vaulted over docks and ran through the water's edge around fences. Lucy and Mel overtook Ben again; Mel had her prize firmly clenched in her teeth. The last dock before a peninsula of reeds was ahead of Ben; Melanie and Lucy bounded through the reeds and splashed into the water on the other side. Ben tripped as he vaulted over the dock and heard his pursuers' voices getting closer. They would see him if he stood up, so he crawled under the dock and out into the water. He trod through the muddy bottom under the dock until it was deep enough to hide him. He was under the pier in neck-high water with the dock six inches over the water line. He kept his head tilted back so he could breathe, peering through the spaces between the planks above. He could hear the dealers saying.

"You see them?"

"They can't be far; those reeds are flattened check in there."

He heard one making his way through the reeds, and the other walked out on the dock most likely to get a better view of the shoreline. Ben stood in the murky water as he watched the shoes of his pursuer walking on the dock directly over his face. Ben quieted his breath still gasping for air from their frenzied escape. He hoped the dogs would not double back and be hurt by these two thugs.

"You see them?" The jacketed one called from the dock.

"No sign of them. There's a street through this yard so they must have made it to the street," the other said.

"Let's get back to the car. We can cover more ground that way. I'm gonna kill him and his dogs when I get him," the jacketed one cursed.

Manuel's feet passed back over Ben heading toward the shore. He heard the younger dealer pushing back through the reeds. Ben poked his head out to see them walking through the backyard of the adjacent house to the street. His heart was still pounding, the escape was too close for comfort, and he wondered where his dogs went. Ben waited several minutes to give his pursuers enough time to leave. He had to find Lucy and Melanie and stay away from the streets where the goons would be looking for him. He was wet again, so he just waded through the water and around the peninsula. On the other side were more bay homes with their associated docks and small beaches. There was no sight of Melanie and Lucy. Ben walked and swam a little around the small marina south of the homes past the restaurants on the bay. He passed the bar's volleyball court and around their overhanging decks to Que Pasa's beach with tables. There were no goons in sight. At Que Pasa's beach, he saw Melanie paddling in the water chasing seabirds nesting under the deck, and Lucy was digging at one of several holes on the beach. If he weren't so glad to see them, he would have scolded them both. He called them to him as he trudged onto the beach at Que Pasa. They came happily; wagging their tails, and there was no sign of the bag.

"Melanie, where's the bag girl? Get the bag," he coaxed her. She bounded into the bay after another seabird, "No, Mel, not the birds, the bag," he said thinking he was wasting his time. "What a dumb dog," he thought. Ben sat down at a table weighing his options. The waitress noticed the wet patron and asked him if he wanted a drink.

"No thanks," he replied.

Ben didn't have any money even if he wanted one. He could use a stiff drink to calm his nerves. He couldn't go back to the condo because they would be sure to be watching it. He was not a happy camper, his car keys, wallet, and clothes were in the apartment. "What a mess I've gotten into" he thought. All this trouble over a bag of drugs and money that Melanie made vanish as quickly as it appeared. He wondered how he would explain all this to the police.

Chapter 18

No sooner did the thought cross his mind when he saw a police car patrolling Que Pasa's parking lot. Ben charged around Que Pasa's bar. He ran, flagging down the vehicle. The officer saw him running behind his cruiser and stopped. Ben was out of breath again and started babbling, "Officer two guys, drug dealers I think, my dog found a bag of money, they're after me, he had a gun…"

"Whoa, whoa, slow down, partner," the officer said. "Take a breath and tell me what's troubling you."

He swallowed, took a deep breath, and collected his thoughts. He proceeded to tell the officer the story of the bag of drugs and cash and the two men who were after him. The officer looked skeptically at Ben's saturated clothing and disheveled look. The story was so outrageous he considered it may be the truth. Ben appeared to be sincere and more coherent as he continued to speak. The officer radioed for assistance to check out this story of drug dealers and guns. Within five minutes two additional patrol cars pulled up. Ben repeated his story and speculated the bag was most likely somewhere in the bay.

"Sir, do you know the men who were chasing you?" the lead officer asked.

"No, but I can identify them if I see them," he replied.

"Do you know where they live, sir?"

"No, but I have a general idea, it's in one of the condos at the end of Dagworthy street facing the beach," Ben replied.

"Are there any witnesses to this assault?" he questioned further.

"No, sir, but my girlfriend did see the bag," he replied.

"Where's your girlfriend now?" he asked.

"I don't know; she's on her way back to New Jersey. She left for her home about forty minutes ago."

"You say the dog lost the bag of evidence. Where did you see it last?" he asked. "It's unlikely we will be able to build a case without the bag or witnesses," he added

"On Dagworthy as I ran from the man with the gun; my dog Melanie grabbed it and carried it to the bay." Ben added, "I don't know what happened to it after that. My dogs, I almost forgot about my dogs." Ben said as he headed back around Que Pasa to the dining beach with the officers following. Melanie was back in the water chasing the nesting birds from under the deck, and Lucy was digging another hole in the sand. Ben called Melanie. She bounded through the water onto the small beach where she proceeded to dig in the hole Lucy was fixated on. It was rapidly becoming a reasonably deep hole as Ben stared at the progress the two dogs were making.

"The holes; Mel likes to bury her toys in holes. Maybe the bag is here," Ben said crazily. He dropped to his knees at the hole the two were digging and joined then in their furious digging. He started to scoop sand out of the first hole with his hands. Finding nothing, he moved to the next. Ben looked like a madman to the police. He knelt and dug with his wet clothes covered in sand. Not finding the bag he moved again into the third hole when a small girl about four years old walked over. Melanie became bored watching Ben dig and began her cinnamon donut routine in the sand.

"Hey, mister, are those your dogs?" she said pointing to Melanie and Lucy.

"Yes," he answered.

"Can I pet them?" she asked.

"Yes," Ben answered as he moved over to the fourth area of disturbed sand. The officers just looked at him with a mixture of pity and concern for his mental status. He started digging again with his bare hands, his fingers becoming raw and bleeding from the pieces of shells.

"Hey, mister, what are you looking for?" the girl asked.

"Nothing," Ben replied. "Maybe you should go back to your mommy now," he added.

"My daddy is here; he's the bartender. I came to work with him today," she replied.

"How nice," he said as he continued his frantic digging.

"Your dog dug his bone over there," she said pointing to a side table.

"Huh? Are you talking about the fuzzy beige dog?" Ben asked.

"The funny big one," she said pointing to Melanie. "He dug his bone over there. Are you looking for his bone?"

"Yes, sweetheart, show me where she dug her bone," Ben encouraged her.

She took him by the hand and led him to an end table; the officers looked quite interested in this surprising development and followed.

"Right there," she said pointing to some disturbed sand around and under the table. "The doggie buried her bone there."

Ben dropped to his knees and started digging furiously; the youngest of the three officers bent over and started to help. A few inches down they uncovered the blue handle of the bag. The officer grabbed and yanked the missing bag of cash out of the sand.

"Well I'll be…." the older of the officers said.

"You're such a smart little girl," Ben said jubilantly as he picked her up and hugged her. The bartender came running now aware of the commotion surrounding his child.

"Hey, what're you doing with my daughter?" he said protectively.

"Everything is alright, sir; your daughter is safe. I think she just found some crucial evidence for us," the younger officer comforted the dad.

"I think she's earned a big reward from me," Ben added. "Your daughter has saved my day."

He stared with a confused look as the officers inspected the bag.

"A lot of money and a large quantity of a white powdery substance; it validates his story," the younger officer added.

Melanie had wandered over to inspect the now bagless hole as she started to shake covering the group of officers with a fine coating of wet sand.

Chapter 19

Manuel and Vinny drove around the streets of Dewey looking for their elusive bag. There was the typical migration of beachgoers walking toward the shore. Bathing suit-clad families toting wagons loaded with children, beach chairs, umbrellas, towels and assorted sundries as their older children swung pails and shovels running ahead in anticipation of a day in the sand. Teenagers and college students in skimpy bikinis and board shorts carried chairs and wave boards as they joked and laughed on the way to the surf. With no sight of Ben and the dogs, they swung around and rechecked Ben's condo. Manuel went up as Vinny waited in the car. The condo door was still ajar, and there were no signs that his man had returned. He checked the bedroom and found Ben's clothing in the drawers and his wallet and keys on the dresser. Manuel pocketed the keys and wallet. He now had some information on his dog guy and was making sure Ben could not use his car to get out of town or have any available financial means for escape. He rechecked the kitchen closet where the bag was initially found. Having no success, Manuel headed back to his car and jumped in.

"Any sign of him?" Vinny asked.

"No, but I have his car keys and wallet; he isn't going far," Manuel added.

They drove to check the center of town by the restaurants. In the parking lot of Que Pasa, they saw the three police cruisers. This was not a beneficial development for them. Manuel had hoped Ben would take the dogs and the bag and go underground for a while. It would have given him time to trace Ben's location and finally retrieve his money. He assumed Ben had panicked and must have called the police. Manuel had a big shipment scheduled to be boated in this evening. It was a new and very nervous supplier, and Manuel had given him his personal assurances that all would go smoothly. He had to make the transaction.

"Vinny, we better forget about the bag and count our losses," Manuel stated.

"But the bag had my stash in it," Vinny whined back.

"Forget your stash; the load coming in has a thousand of your stashes in it. I'll cut some out for you. Let's get to the marina and out to the rendez-vous spot. We can grab some heroes and beer, and we can do some fishing until they get in. I'll have

Maria close up the condo and send her home. Once we get the shipment, we can take the boat to our Ocean City dock and let the missing bag blow over. There's nothing to tie it to us. I guess I can't use the Delaware condo for a while. What a shame. It's a great spot, and I joined that expensive yacht club with the crappy bar," Manuel explained.

"You can let me use it; I love the beach," Vinny said enthusiastically.

"No one is gonna use the condo for a long while, especially us, unless you have a wish for some jail time," he added.

"Yeah, I got it. No condo," Vinny said with a frown.

Chapter 20

The older officer informed Ben he would need to make a statement and look at some mug shots at the station.

"Fine with me," Ben stated. He figured the station was the safest place to be with the two thugs looking for him

"I need to take the dogs," he added.

"We can call animal services. They'll hold the dogs for you," the older officer said.

"No way! The dogs go with me," Ben protested.

Ben insisted they either take the dogs or he would refuse to cooperate. He came to an agreement with the officers; the dogs would come with them, but they had to stay in the car. Ben had forgotten the local station was closed, so they were off to Dover's police station. Ben suggested the dogs could stay in the car with the air conditioning running. Cops left their cars idling for hours, and they could do it for the dogs. On the way to Dover, they passed the shopping district. Ben convinced the officer to stop at a pet mart so he could buy some leashes and treats for the dogs and at a burger joint so he could get some lunch. The officer was annoyed with the stops and even more annoyed when Ben asked to borrow the money from him. Ben had left everything in the condo and explained to the officer it this was an unexpected trip.

"Thanks," Ben told him. "I'll pay you back once I get back to the condo." Ben bought two new leashes and a hamburger and fries for himself and a cheeseburger for Melanie and Lucy. The trio sat in the back of the police cruiser eating on the way to Dover. After Ben and dogs wolfed down their lunch, Lucy sat contently in Ben's lap watching the passing countryside. Mel huddled against the door and started drooling. It would have been a two-hour trip with the weekend beach traffic; luckily the patrol car had lights and sirens. The weaving around slow-moving traffic unnerved Mel and increased her drool. She started to gag. Lucy saw it coming and leaned away from Melanie.

"How much longer to Dover?" Ben inquired.

"We are entering the city limits; just another five minutes," the officer answered.

Before Ben could ask the officer to pull over, Mel wretched and threw up her lunch on the back seat of the cruiser. Lucy climbed up onto Ben to avoid the overspray. The front passenger seat was blocked by a Plexiglas shield preventing Lucy's escape. The officer turned to see what the commotion was.

"My car, put something under her," he said as Melanie spewed another round of burger. Ben looked frantically for something to put under Melanie. Ben apologized that there was nothing to catch the vomit even if he had been fast enough. The seat and floor of the patrol car were a mess. They arrived at the parking lot of the station.

"Don't worry, I'll clean it up," Ben promised.

"It's going to stink back there," the officer said as he opened the back door of the cruiser for Ben. Melanie began to gobble down the pieces of burger she just vomited up.

"It may be clean faster than you think," Ben added.

"Dumb freaking dog," the officer said.

"Yeah, dumb dog," Ben repeated.

Ben made sure the officer left the motor running and the air conditioner on. He did not want two dead dogs. Ben wet some paper towels in the bathroom of the station and cleaned the remaining vomit the best he could. Lucy looked at him with her soulful eyes, begging not to be left in a car with Melanie.

"Sorry, Lucy, I think Mel is done," and to Mel, he said, "Mel, no more throwing up please."

Chapter 21

In the station, Ben met with the lead detective Myers, and a stenographer in a conference-size room with a small table, two chairs, and a small desk where the stenographer sat. The room was conspicuously absent of other furniture or any clutter. The far wall was mirrored; Ben suspected it was the stereotypical one-way glass. The inspector brought him some coffee and proceeded to guide Ben through his story, occasionally interrupting to extract a fact or explore something he said in greater depth. He was well practiced at extracting a tale and inconspicuously made Ben repeat and reword to verify his facts were straight. Ben had no anxiety about the interrogation since he told only the incidents as they happened. He grew tired and daydreamed. He started to imagine himself as a jewel thief under questioning when a second well-dressed man entered the room toting a chair. He pulled Ben out of his fantasy and back to reality when he introduced himself as FBI Agent Freeman. He wore a dark grey pinstripe Armani suit with a faint blue pinstripe, and a blue shirt with a white collar.

His tie was a matching blue and grey horizontal stripe. His suit was impeccably tailored; it fit him like a glove.

"FBI, this must be big," Ben announced.

"Mr. Grece, it's always big when drugs are involved," the agent said.

He apologized for his not being present for his initial report and asked Ben if he wouldn't mind reviewing a few facts with him. Ben learned in the conversation that he was dispatched from Maryland. He made Ben repeat the entire chain of events.

"We have photographs of some people of interest we would like you to view," Agent Freeman said.

"Sure," Ben replied.

Agent Freeman informed him the men in the photos were all involved in interstate drug trafficking, hence the FBI involvement. Ben flipped through the images, surprised at how many different people there were. The drug trade must be booming. He came to a picture of the jacket man sitting at a restaurant table in some tropical setting with the same woman he had seen him with at Que Pasa.

"Here, this is the one that was in my condo with a gun. I also saw him the night before with this woman at Que Pasa, the restaurant in Dewey." Ben said.

"Interesting, are you sure this is the man you saw?" he asked

"When someone points a gun at you they become unforgettable," Ben replied.

The door opened, and another well-dressed man entered the room and huddled with Agent Freeman and Detective Myers. They were discussing the man Ben identified in the photo. There was amazement in the new agent's voice. Ben overheard parts of the conversation: "We should move now" and "Canvas the neighborhood." Detective Myers and the other presumed agent left the room, and Agent Freeman returned to Ben.

"Mr. Grece, this has presented a unique opportunity for us. The man you identified is of extreme interest to the bureau. He is Manuel Garcia, and we have him as second in drug trafficking from the Jersey shore to Florida. If we can tie the bag to him, coupled with kidnapping and attempted murder, we could put him away for a long time. I hope we can count on your cooperation."

"As long as you can assure my safety, I'll try to do whatever I can," Ben said.

"You are safe with us Mr. Grece; if you're up to it, I want you to show me where exactly you found the bag. I have the entire area under surveillance, so a precise location will help," Agent Freeman said.

"It's on Dewey Beach, Dagworthy Street. I would like to get back to my dogs. The dogs need a walk if it's okay with you?" he asked.

"Sure, I like dogs," Agent Freeman replied.

Ben and the agent returned to the cruiser. It was hot, and he was relieved to see the interior of the car was almost cold. "Good thing the cruiser didn't overheat in this weather," he thought. Lucy was sleeping on the clean side, and Mel was curled up over the vomit spot.

"Grab the dogs, we'll take my car," Agent Freeman said.

"Okay," Ben said as he leashed the dogs and walked them along the grass fringe of the parking lot. Once they had relieved themselves, he led them to the back seat of Agent Freeman's car. Here we go again, he thought, and Freeman had such a nice new car. Luckily the ride was fast and uneventful. Melanie didn't have anything left in her stomach to throw up. It was nearing five o'clock. The day was a blur of activity and crazy events. Ben told the agent he wanted to stop at the condo. He needed some dry clothes; his groin was starting to chafe from his bay water dampened underwear. He also needed to give the dogs some food and water and to get the money he owed the patrolman. The condo door was still open.

"Take the dogs back down and wait on the side of the building behind the shrubs," Agent Freeman ordered Ben, and he drew his weapon and stood against the door frame peering into the condo. Ben saw him nudge the door open the rest of the way as he entered gun at the ready. Agent Freeman made a security sweep of the rooms in the condo before re-appearing.

"Okay, Ben, bring the dogs up; the condo is clear."

Ben was relieved and impressed with the professional way the agent did his job.

"Sorry, I didn't mean to scare you. I didn't want to walk in on Mr. Garcia or one of his thugs waiting in the condo for you."

In the condo, Ben suggested the agent change into something less conspicuous than a suit. Detective Freeman was close to Ben's size, so he offered some sweatpants and a t-shirt. The agent declined. Ben went into the bedroom to change and noticed his wallet and keys were missing. He had left them on the dresser before Manuel accosted him and now they were gone.

Ben reported to the agent his wallet and car keys were missing. Ben speculated the drug dealers must have come back and taken them. Agent Freeman assured him he would have the car keys replaced. Ben found the spare key to the condo which the agent took and promised to have a new set made for Ben. He assured Ben that all his wallet's contents could be replaced. Ben fed and watched as his dogs drank two dishes of water. He thought they must have been dehydrating in the police car. He felt some pangs of guilt. It was after five and Ben figured he could let the dogs run on the beach; after all, he had FBI protection now and assumed the thugs would stay far away from the man in the suit. Ben pondered how stupidly conspicuous they would look. Ben guessed it was safer for him to be seen with a visible agent rather than a disguised one.

Chapter 22

Ben walked with Agent Freeman pointing out where the thugs chased him and how he ended up at Que Pasa with the dogs. They walked down across the main street to the beach block. The dogs were pulling, anxious to get on the beach. Ben mentioned letting the dogs run on the beach to Agent Freeman, but the agent thought it a bad idea to be out on the beach. "Too much visibility," he said. Ben knew he was right. He couldn't help thinking they would be visible because of the man in the suit among the bathing-suited, shorts, and t-shirt-wearing beach revelers, not because of him and the dogs. They came to the stairs, and Ben showed him where Melanie appeared with the bag and speculated it was from one of the adjoining beachfront condos that shared the decks. Melanie started barking and kept pulling to the beach entrance.

"No, no, heel, Melanie, heel," Melanie had no interest in listening; she lunged again at the end of her leash, causing Ben to slip and fall on the sandy pavement. He let go of the strap and Melanie bounded barking onto the beach.

"No, girl, come," Ben shouted futilely as Melanie ran to the waterfront.

"Get your dog," the agent said in a very annoyed tone.

Ben raised himself to his feet and as he brushed the sand off his hands, turned with Lucy and ran down the beach after Melanie. The chocolate Lab and his owner were in their usual spot. The Lab was out swimming toward his toy. Melanie without hesitation headed straight into the water, leaping leash and all over a breaking wave and into the breaking crest of a wave directly behind the first and disappeared into the foam. "Great," Ben thought, "I have nice dry clothes on." He released Lucy and dove into the foam Melanie had disappeared into. The ocean was very rough, and Ben tried to keep his head up looking for Melanie's head to appear. He was slammed by another wave that took him off his feet. Ben found himself twirling helplessly in the surf. Melanie bumped against his back as they swirled in the chaos of the wave. Ben felt the leash on his side and wrapped it in his hand. The surge pulled him deeper. He was slammed into the sand, knocking the breath out of his burning lungs. He tried to gasp for some air, only liquid filled his mouth. His throat and chest convulsed as the roar of the wave quieted, and he felt himself weightless floating in a dark abyss.

Ben felt someone lift him up and, with a sudden jolt, he was slammed down onto the sand. There was air again. He lay coughing, spitting up water from his very depths. He heard Melanie's seal bark and felt the leash in his hand. Funny, he had a seal bark too. His chest hurt too much to laugh at himself.

"What just happened?" he squeaked out in a hoarse voice.

"You nearly drowned, you're lucky I followed you on the beach," Agent Freeman said.

His eyes were clearing as he stared up at a wholly saturated Armani suit.

"Oh my God, your suit is ruined," Ben said embarrassed.

"You almost took me down with you. I thought you had an anchor attached, but it was the dog. You had her leash wrapped around your hand. Good thing, too, I don't think the dog would have survived those waves," the agent said.

Ben sat up. "Mel, is Mel alright?" Melanie was again barking with a hoarse bark at the water. He peered out on the horizon. About one hundred yards from the beach was a mid-size yacht and an approaching cigar boat. Mel continued to restlessly bark, and she seemed ready to jump back into the deep. Ben grabbed her leash.

"What's wrong girl? You're acting very strange," he commented.

A beach patrol on a four-wheeler pulled up asking, "Is there a problem here?"

Agent Freeman had also noticed the pair of boats and was staring into the horizon.

"FBI, do you have a pair of binoculars?" Agent Freeman asked as he flashed a wet billfold and badge.

"Sure," the beach patrol said as they handed their binoculars to this wet-suited FBI agent with a quizzical look.

Agent Freemen put the binoculars to his eyes and after peering at the two boats for a minute stated, "Well I'll be, there's our boy, Garcia, fishing."

He pulled out his cell phone noting it was dead, as water dripped out of the earphone port.

The agent asked to borrow the patrol's portable radio and after identifying himself requested a coast guard cutter and helicopter.

"That's some dog you got there," the agent said.

"Dumb dog," the owner of the Lab stated.

"Maybe not so dumb," Ben said back.

Chapter 23

Manuel was at the stern of his boat holding his deep-sea reel. He and Vinny sat fishing for fluke while eating deli sandwiches with a cold beer as they waited for Jose Spinozza, their new contact. They had caught five flukes already, all extremely large and massive. Manuel had never landed such large fish and kept fishing even when the supplier's boat arrived and tied up next to his. Manuel and Vinny greeted their new supplier as he pulled his boat alongside theirs. He had the cocaine as promised stacked in neat bundles in the stern of his cigar boat.

"Manuel, just as I promised you, the best coke you're ever going to find," Jose shouted as he tied his boat to Manuel's.

"Don't yell, you're gonna scare the fish," Manuel rumbled back as he intently stared at the tip of his fishing pole.

Jose climbed into Manual's boat.

"Have a beer," Manuel said as he flipped Jose a bottle. "Vinny, get the suitcase, I'm sure Jose wants to see his money."

Vinny went below to the cabin and emerged carrying the suitcase with the half a million dollars. He handed it to Manuel just as Manuel's pole dipped.

"Whoa, show him the money, Vinny. Crap! I think this is a big one," Manuel said as he struggled to reel in a fish. He was furiously reeling as Vinny opened the suitcase to show Jose the stacks of hundreds it contained. "It's all there amigo, we'll make you a wealthy man if you stick with us," Manuel said as he flipped a huge fluke on the deck of the boat. "Holy crap, look at that fish," he added as the fish flopped around the deck. Jose jumped back as it knocked the suitcase over spilling stacks of bills onto the floor. Manuel laughed as Vinny scrambled to return the cash to the bag. Vinny pulled a gun out of his belt as Jose's eyes widened and he pressed himself back against the rails of the boat.

"Whoa, whoa, what are you doing with that gun? Have you lost your mind?" Manuel yelled.

"I gonna shoot that fish before it bites someone," Vinny said as he pointed his nine-millimeter at the colossal fluke flopping wildly on the deck of the boat.

"Put that gun away! You scared the crap out of Jose, and you're going to put a hole in my boat," Manuel barked at him.

"I guess," Vinny said sheepishly as he shoved the gun back in his pants. "Sorry, Jose, I didn't mean to rattle your cage."

"Vinny, check the shipment," Manuel commanded as he stepped on the considerable fluke and punched it as he bent over.

"There, one calm fish," he said as he laughed.

Jose looked on with a mix of fear and amusement.

Vinny hopped into the cigar boat, slipped his knife blade into one of the bundles and spread the powder on his gums.

"It looks good, high quality," Vinny shouted to Manuel.

Vinny was about to climb back into his boat when he saw the Coast Guard cutter in the distance.

"Manuel, we have a problem. Coastguard."

"Crap, I'm out of here," Jose said as the two men swapped back to their boats.

"Vinny, stash the money in the engine compartment and throw that gun over."

Vinny quickly threw his gun over the side and grabbed the suitcase. He proceeded to stuff the stacks of money next to the motor as Manuel threw Jose's lines into his cigar boat as it powered up and took off.

Manuel flipped his snub nose over the side and grabbed his fishing pole. He sat down as he dropped a line back into the water.

"Vinny, grab a pole and be cool. They got nothing on us."

The two men waved as the Coast Guard approached.

Ben watched a small drama play out; with the approach of the Coast Guard cutter the cigar boat powered up and took off. He observed the Coast Guard board the fishing boat and take two men off in handcuffs. They were two innocent fishermen, as they said.

Chapter 24

Jose headed out to open sea, full throttle. Jose was relieved when he saw the cutter pull alongside Manuel's boat rather than chase him. Manuel's ship and the cutter were shrinking from sight. He sat back in his captain's chair with a wave of relief running through him. He sat enjoying the breeze and ocean spray as his boat cut through the waves. Then he thought he heard another noise over the droning of his engines. He peered around into the sky suspecting the sound of a helicopter in the distance. A dot on the horizon grew larger and larger until the distinct orange striping of the Coast Guard insignia was apparent on the aircraft. Jose started to dump his precious cargo bundle by bundle into the pearl blue seas. Half a million dollars was gone in a matter of two minutes. The helicopter quickly caught up with the speeding boat and positioned itself just in front of his bow. The booming amplified voice of the pilot ordered Jose to stop and come about.

With his cargo consigned to the deep, Jose powered down as he noticed another boat appear on the coastward horizon. A second Coast Guard cutter was heading straight to his location. The helicopter guided the Coast Guard cutter to the cigar boat. The helicopter crew had deployed a buoy on the way to the cigar boat where they saw the bundles being dumped. Once the cutter had boarded the vessel and arrested Jose on suspicion of drug smuggling, the helicopter returned to the beacon in the buoy, and a diver was able to recover most of the contraband bundles. Within an hour and a half, the FBI was informed they had the cigar boat in custody. Ben doubted they needed his testimony after it was announced the Coast Guard, along with the FBI, had made the largest drug bust in Delaware history. The FBI, DEA, and Coast Guard hauled in one hundred kilos of pure cocaine and a half million dollars in cash. It was estimated to have a street value of over nine million dollars. Manuel and Vinny were charged with drug trafficking, racketeering, conspiracy, kidnapping, and attempted murder. Ben was free to go home after an exciting evening of cops and robbers. He had his fill of criminals. Ben told Agent Freeman, "I don't know how to thank you for saving Melanie and me."

"No thanks are needed, I was just doing my job," he replied.

As the agent spoke, Melanie went into her cinnamon donut routine, rolling in the sand. Ben shook hands with the agent just as Melanie shook and pep-pered them both with a fine coating of sand. Ben couldn't help but laugh as he stared at the agent in his sand covered, wet Armani suit.

"At the very least let me buy you a new suit," Ben said to his wet sandy savior.

"Thanks for the offer but it's not necessary. Just promise to keep your dog out of the ocean and warn me in advance of any beach you intend to vacation at," he added.

They shared a hearty laugh as they said farewells.

Chapter 25

Ben packed his stuff and was relieved to be heading back home. It was just two days, and it felt like he had been the shore for an eternity. Ben returned with his exhausted dogs to the condo. Agent Freeman arranged replacement keys for Ben's car. A state trooper delivered the keys to him within an hour. Ben was amazed; it would have taken him days to replace the keys, or he would have had to replace the locks in the car. He was given a voucher for a local gas station; luckily Manuel had not seen his cell phone on the night table. He gave Melanie her Dramamine and packed the bags and gear into the car. Ben stripped the beds and bagged the dirty sheets and placed them on the porch for the laundry service. He herded the dogs into the car and made them comfortable in the back seat. Ben fired up the engine and headed down the block. The condo was shrinking in his rearview mirror and, as he rounded the corner onto Route 1, a feeling of relief washed over him. They were on the way home. Ben's cell phone rang. He picked it up on the hands-free; it was the Chief.

"Hey Ben, sorry I'm so late getting back to you. I had my physical, and on the way back someone robbed the quick mart in town," he said.

"Is everyone all right?" Ben asked.

"Yes, Officer Banks chased him to Overlook Park, and we called in the dogs and found him a little over an hour ago. He surrendered without a fight," the chief told him.

"What can I do for you?" the chief added.

"Nothing at the moment. I have a story to tell you when I get back into town. I'm on my way home now. Let's have coffee in the morning, and I'll fill you in," Ben said.

"Sounds good to me, I'll see you tomorrow," the Chief said as he hung up.

Ben was making good time traveling home, and he lectured his Melanie, "Next time we stay on the bay; I think we've both had enough ocean for a lifetime."

He turned to look at Mel just in time to see her throw up all over the back seat. Lucy sprinted over the seat to the front passenger seat as Melanie continued to gag. He smiled to himself as he thought, "Dumb dog, no, just my dog. It doesn't get much better than this."

The two dogs whined as Ben pulled into his driveway. It was three in the morning. Ben wasn't sure who was happier, him or the dogs. He left his bags in the car, and he was followed by his bounding dogs. They entered the house and headed straight to bed. The dogs curled on their pillows and Ben barely remembered his head hitting his pillow. The trio slept until noon before the dogs woke him to take their walk. Ben felt safe again and at peace with the world as he walked the familiar blocks with his loyal dogs. The dogs seemed more at ease as they sniffed the familiar scents of the neighborhood. It was an adventure Ben would not soon forget. Ben met the Chief for coffee after his walk and spun a tale that amazed the Chief.

"Holy cow, Ben, the name Manuel Garcia is well known among law enforcement on the East Coast. You're lucky not to have been shot or injured."

"Chief, it was crazy; I still cannot believe all that transpired from my Melanie snatching the drug dealer's bag. It could be the plot for a movie."

"A dangerous series of events; he is a real bad man, and this is real life crime, Ben."

Chapter 26

Manuel's trial proceeded over the course of several months. Agent Freeman kept Ben updated as to the progress of proceedings. Ben also followed the story in the *New York Times*. In the series of articles that ran over the ensuing weeks about Manuel Garcia, Ben was made aware of how large a crime figure Manuel was. The stories detailed the connections Manuel had to organized crime on the East Coast. He had the persona of a significant boss. The more Ben read, the more uneasy he was about his involvement in the trial. Agent Freeman continued to assure him he was safe and of the importance of his testimony to ensure that Manuel would never see daylight again.

Ben was scheduled to testify almost five months later. He was extremely anxious about the proceedings. The FBI arranged car service and a hotel for his testimony in the Federal Court in Dover, Delaware. Sandy had shown up at his doorstep the week he returned from the beach and moved back in as if nothing had happened. She was charged with watching the dogs for the two days Ben would be in

Dover. He was the first witness scheduled in the morning. The FBI general counsel reviewed his testimony with him over a pleasant supper at the hotel the night before. Ben found himself dry mouthed and sweating as the courtroom filled. Manuel Garcia entered the room with an entourage of lawyers. Manuel, upon seeing Ben, kept his gaze on him with a coy smile on his face. His stare unnerved Ben. The general council reassured Ben that everything would be fine. Ben, in spite of being very nervous, was pleased his testimony was straightforward and very short. The defense spent less than ten minutes on his cross-examination. Manuel glared at Ben the entire time he was testifying. Ben was dismissed and allowed to return home. The jury was out for less than one hour. They found him guilty on all counts. Manuel Garcia was sentenced to forty years without parole on a laundry list of charges. Ben felt safer knowing Manuel would be behind bars for what may be the rest of his natural life. Ben settled back into the daily routine of his life happy with the knowledge that the Manuel chapter was now behind him.

Manuel may have been confined, but his influence extended far beyond his jail cell. With a bottomless bank account, Manuel was able to procure all the comforts that he was accustomed to. He was transferred to a private cubicle where his queen-sized memory foam mattress awaited him. He was given a high definition big screen television with full cable access. He was also granted internet and cell phone privilege. His private bath was well appointed with all the necessary grooming needs. From an outsider's perspective, Manuel had everything he needed except his freedom, but the fact of his incarceration burned in Manuel's gut. To think some moron and his dog from New Jersey ruined his life. Manuel had it all, money, women, and drugs with a growing sphere of power and influence. His syndicate was growing and just when he thought he had it all, a bumbling dog put him in jail. Manuel spread the word among the New Jersey streets that he wanted revenge and was willing to pay. Word spread to Sergio, a small time credit card thief and the strong arm for his brother, Vic, a talented computer programmer turned identity thief.

Part II
The Dog Fight

Chapter 27

Ben's downward spiral started innocently enough. It was a lovely spring afternoon, and Lucy and Melanie wanted to go for a walk. Ben leashed them up, and as he opened the door, Sandy yelled she was going to walk with him. She met him at the door and put on a light sweater as she stepped out into the sunshine.

"It's comfortable out; I don't think you need the sweater."

"It's still chilly; you should wear a sweatshirt yourself," she said.

"I'm good, it's beautiful out," Ben added as he walked the dogs down the stairs of the stoop across the lawn to the street. Sandy grabbed Melanie's leash as she stepped into the street. "You're with me today, Mel," and patted her on the head. They took a leisurely stroll around the block; Lucy was happy and prancing the entire way. Melanie lumbered along nose to the ground as was her habit. How could anyone not love a day like this? The sun was heating Ben's face, and the grass and spring flowers were waking from their winter sleep. Daffodils were in bloom, and the hyacinths and tulips were racing behind them ready to usher in a cornucopia of colors and scents. Everyone's property was awash with green and new life. Lucy and Melanie loved to go on their walks almost as much as Ben loved taking them. They would sniff the bushes and shrubbery around the neighborhood and Ben would inhale the clean, fresh air. His spirits would soar with each passing block as they met neighbors and chatted along the way. Lucy would greet everyone – person, and dog alike – with a great fondness and love for being alive. She seemed to pull the day's mood up to new heights. Mel, if in the mood, might bowl a neighbor down with her enthusiastic greeting or just ignore them. Even Sandy would be cheerful and happy on their walks. The pure pleasure of walking a dog was infectious.

They were passing the latest mc-mansion, a gaudy monstrosity built on a lot designed for a modest house. The split level that once stood there belonged to an old widow, Mrs. Hendricks. It was a quaint home with beige clapboard and pink shutters. It was ringed with a well-kept white picket fence. It was warm and inviting. Mrs. Hendricks was quite the gardener; she had a beautiful bulb garden along the fence line and flowering azaleas and rhododendrons along the foundation. There was a flowering cherry on one side of the property and a beautiful red maple on the other. The house was razed, and the gardens bulldozed to make way for this stone castle complete with parapets and towers. The trees and flowers were gone, and the sizeable uninspired shrubbery was conspicuously planted to block light from the dark shaded windows on the lower floor of the new house. It was a stark contrast to the beautiful, brightly colored curtains in the previous home. The mc-mansion stood out like a sore thumb. How the town's planning board could allow such a hideous abode was beyond Ben. This extravagant home always appeared empty but an occasional lighted room suggesting some type of habitation. It had none of the characteristics of a home, no children playing, no toys in the driveway, and no signs of life generally.

The cold stone, mahogany front door, and lack of light made one think of a mausoleum, not a house. Ben wondered who wanted to own such a huge house and never be home.

Today someone was home. The gaudy front door opened and out stepped a middle-aged man with a small black and white Boston terrier running out next to him. He wore tight black jeans and a tight-fitting black t-shirt. He was sockless with black boat shoes. His hair was jet black and gelled back, and he sported a chin strap type beard. He was Vic Pola-koff, a computer troubleshooter. He saw Ben and the dogs. This was the guy his brother Sergio told him about. It was his luck that he lived in the same neighborhood. The word was there's a big bounty on the guy's head if Vic wanted the job. Vic was into internet and credit card theft and was leery about taking on the project. Sergio convinced him that they could make a name for themselves in the syndicate by taking Ben down. Vic was amused; he had just heard about the bounty and here walking down the block was his target. Vic looked down at his dog, "Get 'em," he told Max.

The terrier headed straight to Lucy with teeth snarling and fur up on his back. Lucy didn't know what hit her. Melanie pulled back as the terrier at-tacked Lucy; she pulled her leash out of Sandy's hand and ran through the adjoining yard, tail be-tween her legs, towards home. The terrier savagely bit at Lucy's neck, Lucy let out horrific yelps and tried to back away. She stumbled against Ben's foot and rolled backward. The terrier was on her, biting into her soft belly trying to disembowel Ben's baby. Lucy let out ear-piercing yelps, and Sandy screamed in horror. Ben looked from Lucy, terrorized and in pain, to Sandy's concerned and horrified face, to the dog's owner for some help. The terrier's owner was calmly looking at the scene. He didn't yell or recall his dog; instead, Ben perceived a smirk on this man's face. He thought it was funny. Ben reacted quickly, screaming, "NO! NO!"

Using his foot, Ben scooped the terrier off Lucy and flung it to the curb. Still screaming "NO!" at the deranged attacker, the Boston terrier retreated back to its owner. He bent over and examined Lucy; Ben shook, and the blood pounded in his head. She was bleeding from several spots. He inspected her as he heard Sandy muttering, "Oh my, is she alright?"

Lucy tried to crawl into his arms.

He comforted Lucy, saying "Its ok girl, you'll be alright."

Vic, with his dog at his side, walked across his lawn, closer to Ben.

Ben heard the terrier's owner say, "You kicked my dog."

He looked up from Lucy, muttering "Huh?" Vic repeated in a rough tone reminiscent of an episode from *The Sopranos*, "You kicked my dog."

Ben replied in an upset voice, "You saw what happened. What did you expect me to do?"

"You kicked my dog," he stated again with a threatening tone.

"I didn't kick your dog. I swept it to the curb, it's not hurt," Ben said.

He picked Lucy up, and she laid her head over his shoulder. She whimpered softly.

"Don't make this into something it's not," Ben added.

"How would you like a beating," the terrier's owner interjected as he moved toward Ben.

His fists were clenched, biceps bulging and veins swelling in his neck. He was slightly taller than Ben and stockier. He appeared to have spent some time around the gym. As he closed the distance between them, Ben felt an adrenaline rush, his trembling worsened, and his stomach flipped over in his gut. He instinctively handed Lucy to Sandy, and as he turned back, he was bumped back by the dog owner's chest. The wind was knocked from his lungs as he caught his balance to prevent a fall backward. A drumbeat in Ben's ears, his entire body shook with the fear that Vic's next move would be to break his jaw. Ben stepped into Vic's next chest thrust with his right fist jumping from his body. Ben heard a voice saying, "Beat me up. We'll see who will beat who," as his fist made contact with Vic's jaw. Oddly enough the voice was his. Vic staggered back, both hands to his face. His jaw stung, and he shook with anger. His face reddened as his rage built. He was about to charge Ben when he noticed his next door neighbor, a nosy old widow, peering with a shocked look, out her bedroom window. Vic knew if he continued she would call the police. The last thing he wanted was to be on the radar of the local police department.

Sandy was screaming at Ben, "What's wrong with you? Stop fighting!"

Vic choked out, "You don't know who you're messing with," backing up slightly, holding his aching jaw.

Ben told Sandy to shut up and turned back to his attacker, glaring at both him and his dog. With a quivering voice, he ordered, "Leave me my dog and alone. You started this; just back off."

Ben grabbed Lucy back into his arms and headed for home to nurse his girl. Behind his back, Vic gurgled, "This ain't over, you're a dead man, you and your dog," as he retreated to his house. Vic turned at the door's threshold and watched amused as Sandy yelled at his shaking prey.

Ben just kept walking as Sandy followed behind droning about what a jerk Ben was and he should be arrested for assault, asking, "Why did you hit that man?"

"Look at Lucy, look at her," Ben screeched. "He thought it was funny and would have done the same to me. Well, I bet he's not laughing now."

"You're a street thug; you hit him," Sandy added.

"That's just great, you saw what happened, and you are blaming me?" Ben asked with consternation. "I guess I should have let him tear me up like his dog did to Lucy."

Chapter 28

Ben walked back to the house in resentful silence worrying about his Lucy. Melanie was there sitting on the front steps with her, "what, me worry?" look. Ben had forgotten about Melanie with all the commotion. He felt pangs of guilt as he approached her. He was so concerned with Lucy's plight, he could have lost Melanie. Sandy stormed past them slamming the door behind her. Ben followed behind with his injured Lucy and Melanie in tow. Once inside Ben went to work inspecting every inch of his baby. Her fur was wet with patches of blood from the attack. Melanie sat next to them shaking as much as Lucy, trying to lick the bleeding wounds as Ben examined them.

Ben told his frightened dog, "No, Mel, stay. Lucy will be alright, good girl," as he pushed Melanie's face away from the wounds. Ben grabbed a couple of gauze pads and dabbed at the areas of blood. He worked the fur apart to assess the damage. Lucy was bleeding from several scratches over her neck and shoulders with a couple of deep bleeding punctures on her belly. Ben looked down at himself; he realized his shirt was covered with blood.

"That bastard and his dog," he muttered to himself.

Sandy was in the basement office stewing over Ben's behavior.

Ben called to her, "Sandy, help me. Lucy's hurt bad; I need help cleaning her wounds."

Sandy ignored his calls. He could not believe Sandy's reaction to the incident. His anger with Sandy was quickly forgotten as he continued to tend to Lucy's injuries. Ben was still shaking and feared that Lucy's wounds may be severe. He attempted to dab the belly wound with a dampened gauze pad but Lucy yelped, and he was too shaken to try it again. He called his vet. The receptionist listened to Ben tell the story of the attack on Lucy. She put Ben on hold while she asked Dr. LoFaro if he could bring her in.

"Don't worry, sir. Dr. LoFaro said to bring her right over," she informed Ben.

"Thank you, thank you," Ben replied to the phone as he hung up.

"Sandy, please, I need help with Lucy. She needs to go to the vet. She's hurt badly," he begged his girlfriend. Silence came back from the basement and Ben had no time to deal with Sandy's mood swings. Ben wrapped Lucy's belly with a towel and gingerly carried his injured princess to the car. He carefully placed her on the back seat; blood spotted the beige seats. Ben paid no attention to the stains; he was focused solely on Lucy's injuries and suffering. He jumped in the front seat saying, "It'll be alright, stay, I'll get you there," as he pulled the car out of the driveway with tears welling up in his eyes.

Chapter 29

Ben arrived at the veterinarian fifteen minutes later. The receptionist took one look at Ben with his blood-stained shirt and Lucy wrapped in the bloody towel and commented, "Oh my." She peered over the counter and saw the blood on Lucy's fur and rushed her right into a treatment room. Dr. LoFaro followed within a minute and went directly to work examining Lucy's wounds. As the doctor parted the blood-clotted fir to investigate the injuries, he glanced up at Ben's horror-stricken face. It was ashen with a pained look as he recounted the attack to the doctor. Ben swayed from side to side as he stared at Lucy's wounds. LoFaro assured Ben her injuries, although deep on her belly, did not appear to be dangerous.

"She was fortunate, Ben," LoFaro informed Ben. "You, on the other hand, had better sit down and relax. Lucy is going to be fine. I don't want you as my next patient," he added with a tone of concern.

"You're right," Ben said as he sat in a side chair. "I'll be alright. I'm just upset. It was such a vicious attack; I can't get it out of my mind. Lucy's screams are still echoing in my head."

The vet explained to Ben that her abdomen was not punctured deep enough to perforate her bowel. He added, "The incisors of the other dog didn't puncture through Lucy's abdominal muscles. The muscles protect the bowel. If the bowels were perforated, she would be at a very high risk of an abdominal infection called peritonitis. Luckily it was not a very large dog that attacked her." He went to work cleaning her wounds and opening instruments. He explained he needed to sew up several of her lacerations. His assistant opened several sterile packages and set up a tray for Dr. LoFaro to work from. The doctor drew up two syringes of a local anesthetic, and as the assistant held Lucy, he proceeded to numb the areas. He commented on how good Lucy was. She flinched a time or two but let the doctor do his work as Ben, and the assistant comforted her. Ben watched as the doctor nimbly punctured and drew the curved suture needle through each side of the wound as he pressed the fur back away from the wound edges. Ben stood up to get a better view of LoFaro's work. The room started to tilt as his stomach developed a hollow feeling. Ben was forced to sit back down, and he bent forward in the chair and lowered his head until the room stopped moving and his nausea passed. He gazed out the window until the doctor had finished his work. A few sutures later and some intra-muscular antibiotics, and the doctor was done. Ben gingerly scooped up his princess of a dog as LoFaro reviewed the aftercare with Ben.

The receptionist waved Ben out the door. "We'll send you a bill. Dr. LoFaro wants you to take Lucy straight home. Ben carried Lucy back to the car and carefully placed her back on the stained rear seat. Lucy and Ben returned home both feeling exhausted. Ben was drained of all energy but was pleased to hear from Sandy the police had not paid them a visit. She was still curt with him, but he decided to let her attitude pass. He felt he and his neighbor were even: Ben's hurt dog for Vic's punch in the jaw. He carried his baby to her dog bed and snuggled her in a blanket. She looked drained too, her soulful eyes stared at her savior, and they seemed to thank him. "Sleep my princess," he whispered, "no one is ever going to hurt you again."

He gently stroked her ears and watched as her eyes grew heavy and she drifted off to sleep. Ben's dogs were his anchor. His affection for them had grown deeper over the years. They gave him the love and attention he couldn't get from his human relationships. His love of Lucy was based on the dog's mothering nature and caring temperament. Ben had never experienced a more giving relationship and from a dog no less. He wished Sandy could be half as nurturing or loving as she. Ben flashed back to the start of their relationship. He considered Sandy his soulmate, she seemed so open and loving, but now it was an empty one-sided relationship. He could not understand where it went so wrong.

Ben spent the week fuming about the incident. Lucy took it all in stride. She was still hurt, and some of her movements were still tentative, but she was able to prance and play with Melanie and her toys. Ben, on the other hand, was resentful of the calloused way his neighbor reacted. He felt his stomach twitch every time he saw Lucy's stitches. Ben could deal with himself being injured, but it upset him when Lucy was hurt. He continued to rant to Sandy about the dog and its owner starting the fight.

Sandy told him "You cannot let things go. Enough already."

He couldn't help it. Lucy was hurt.

Chapter 30

Vic informed Sergio about the incident with the mark Manuel wanted killed. He tried to gain favor with Garcia, but even with his aching jaw, he knew he couldn't kill someone. He instead devised a plan that he thought Garcia would like. The proposal would utilize Vic's computer talents. He had Sergio send a message to Mr. Garcia that he was going to destroy Ben Grece's life starting with his finances. He relayed a detailed plan as to how he would make Ben destitute as a prelude to having him killed. He informed Manuel he was not a killer, but he was capable of making Ben suffer.

Manuel was in his large comfortable cell. The bed, complete with a comforter set, had matching curtains on a barred window on one wall. He was watching a rerun of *The Jersey Shore* on his giant LED television hanging on the other wall. His oak roll top desk and leather chair sat in one corner. He was in his reclining chair when the guard interrupted him to give Vic's message.

"I'm sorry to interrupt, Mr. Garcia," said the guard as he handed him a note with Vic's plan. He sat amused as he read what Vic had in store for Ben. Manuel loved the idea of making Ben suffer as much as possible before his final revenge. Ben had cost him millions, and he had what will be a life sentence if his lawyers couldn't win on appeal. Manuel was confident he would win his appeal once he ensured the outcome of the verdict. He knew that money could buy anything, even a jury: Money talks. He offered Vic half the bounty if he was successful in destroying Ben's life. Once he had suffered enough Manuel would end it. Sergio informed Vic of the offer from Manuel. Vic went to work finding Ben's financial information. He hacked into the town's animal licensing bureau and quickly had all the information he needed, including e-mail, in less than five minutes. Vic knew it would be an unsecured site and would most likely hold a treasure chest full of Ben's sensitive information. Animal licensing was one of the forgotten databases that contained a wealth of unsecured data. It was just waiting for someone to access it.

Vic was the owner of a computer repair company he founded. He studied computer programming and computer repair at a technical school after high school. Vic's talents soon drifted to hacking and viral programming. He partnered with a group of classmates with similar skills. Initially, they hacked for fun, challenging each other into more daring feats. Vic still remembered the thrill the first time he hacked into a secure government site. He dropped a bug into their system that crashed Social Security's servers for three days. It was a front-page story. The group evolved into a credit card and ATM theft ring. It was not nearly as exciting as their hacking challenges but far more profitable.

Chapter 31

Vic sent four e-mails with a keylogger attached to Ben's e-mail address. He called them his fantastic four. Each e-mail was a distinct and different enticement with an embedded link to download the keylogger Vic had programmed. The four e-mails appeared innocuous and enticed even the most suspicious user to click one of them for curiosity's sake. Once clicked, his program did its magic. Silently, with the greatest stealth and anonymity, it added the keylogger designed to send Vic everything his victim typed, including passwords. Vic estimated he had another six to eight months before the antiviral geeks were able to detect and block his logger. He was already in the process of programming the next generation logger. He joked that his motto was, "One step ahead of the geeks." The e-mails were producing a ninety percent return for his theft ring.

Mr. Ben Grece took the bait. Within forty-eight hours Vic had his credit card and bank information. He found out Ben worked for National Bank. Vic acquired his log-in information for his work computer as well as some accounts appearing to be some sort of a stock fund. There were hundreds of millions of dollars in the fund. Vic was amazed and delighted to take the challenge. He knew if he could hack the stock account, there was a lot of money to be had. Those accounts had an advanced security verification system that identified the host computer as well as revolving security identifiers required by the user. Vic had to circumvent the bank's security verifications and could remote log onto Ben's computer when connecting. The system used the host's registered computer as another layer of security, so Vic also needed to layer additional dummy accounts and forwards to cover his tracks. He had to be sure any money transfers would be impossible to trace back to a source. He figured it might take him one or two weeks to prepare. Once done he could remote log through Grece's computer and clean out the stock account.

Vic went right to work; this was turning out to be a challenge worthy of his skills. Vic was going to set Ben up for a grand fall. First, he made copies of the Visa and American Express cards he hacked from Grece's accounts and sent a shopper out with a list of goods. Vic liked high-end electronics, smart flat panel televisions, laptops and quality audio products. These were easy merchandise to unload online. He also instructed his buyer to purchase a gun on his card. He envisioned setting Ben up with the weapon if need be. Once Vic had confirmed the purchases were made, he canceled Ben's cards just to mess with his head. Vic also accessed Ben's online banking services and emptied his checking and savings accounts. The money was wire transferred through several dummy accounts before settling into the last in the line. A runner with false identity would withdraw the money and close the account. Any attempts to trace the money would lead to a cascade of accounts around the country ending in a dead end. The securities account was next.

Chapter 32

Lucy healed without incident and Ben fell back into his daily routine. He returned Lucy to the vet within ten days for her suture removal. She balked at getting her stitches out. She was so traumatized the day of her attack that she let Dr. LoFaro put the sutures in with just local anesthesia, but she was having none of it today. She fought each stitch as Ben held her with the veterinary assistant. The vet and Ben tried to reassure her it would be over soon, but Lucy squirmed the entire time. In spite of her, Dr. LoFaro deftly removed the sutures and placed a dab of bacitracin on each wound. Ben thanked the doctor for his usual excellent work. Dr. LoFaro was a rare and caring professional. He ran a small animal hospital in northern New Jersey. He and his staff loved the pets they cared for. Ben knew he was a comprehensive and skilled vet the first time he met him and trusted him fully when it came to caring for his dogs.

Ben gave the receptionist his Visa card to pay for the service.

"I'm sorry sir your card was declined," she informed Ben.

"Try it again," he said, "I used it the other day without a problem."

She swiped the card again. "Sorry, sir, it still is being declined."

"Is your machine not reading it?" Ben inquired.

"No, sir, it's reading the card; it says declined," she answered.

"I'll have to call them," Ben said as he handed her his American Express and put the Visa card back into his wallet. She swiped and reported the same.

"It must be the machine for both the cards not to work," Ben said.

"I'm sorry, sir, it's not taking it," she said

"No problem, I'll give you a check," he said. Ben paid the bill by check and was off for home with his bandaged Lucy.

The following day Ben stopped at the local hardware store to pick up an air conditioner filter. The days were growing hotter as summer approached, and this year he was determined to be ready. He gave the clerk his Visa card having forgotten about the problem at the vet's office. He had assumed it was their machine anyway; he knew the cards were valid. The clerk informed him his card was declined, and he repeated the process with the American Express with the same results.

"What the... I don't understand why it's not working. I'll have to come back when I get this straightened out," he said. "I'm sorry," Ben added. He quickly exited the store embarrassed and frustrated that his credit cards were being denied.

Chapter 33

Ben went straight home to call his credit card company. Walking in the front door, he was greeted by Lucy, almost back to her usual self. Her tail wagged a hundred miles per hour as she turned her body against him for a pat or a scratch. Melanie lumbered over to get in on the action. Sandy, with her usual cool greeting, informed Ben there were several messages from both American Express and Visa. Ben called Visa first; a pleasant young lady told him there was unusually heavy charging on his account. He asked what the charges were and she rattled off several high-priced transactions he could not have made. She asked Ben if he was in possession of his card. He told her he did and she should freeze the account immediately. She informed him that he had already called and canceled the account three days ago. Ben thanked her and hung up.

"Sandy," Ben bellowed, "did you use my credit card this week?"

"No," she answered.

Sandy had been Ben's girlfriend for over five years, and he knew how she could use a credit card. He had met her at the local mall. He watched as she, loaded with purchases, came down the escalator only to have her cargo tumble down ahead of her. He ran to assist her as she met the packages at the bottom of the escalator. Her momentum awkwardly pushed her onto the bundles. Ben caught her as she fell over her treasures.

"Oh my, I could have broken my neck," she said.

"Right place right time I guess," he said, as he stood her up and gathered up her bags and boxes.

"Quite a load of goods you have here," he added.

"Yes, I did a little shopping today," she said.

Ben would later learn this was a little shopping for her. She was the daughter of the owner of a chain of Doing Donuts. Her family overindulged her, resulting in an extremely spoiled woman. Her occupation was shopper; her job was daddy's money. Ben asked her out as he helped her get her packages into her car. They have been together ever since. They were dating for six months when her dad cut her funds off. Sandy and her dad did not see eye to eye concerning everything from her non-job status to her social arrangement. It was not a problem for Sandy since Ben was available to substitute for her father's role. She moved in and quickly took control of his finances. Ben made a comfortable living and let her spend without protest. A match made by Visa.

Their relationship had become progressively rocky over the past year. It started as most relationships do; there were compromises and considerate attempts to accommodate each other's lifestyle. Over the past years, Sandy had become overbearing and unwilling to compromise. Ben tried to understand her frustration with her father and family. She was apparently upset over being cut off from the family's funds. Her father was strict and extremely stubborn himself. The seed often does not fall far from the tree. Ben has tried to reconcile them with little cooperation from either side. Sandy's relationship with her brothers has become strained in part due to jealousy fueled by her father's favoritism of her brothers. Ben pitied her broken family relationship and has tolerated her mood swings and demands, often to his unhappiness. It had started to take a toll on their relationship. Ben proceeded to call American Express with the same results. Someone charged up a number of high-ticket items and then canceled his card. Ben wondered why the thief canceled the cards. He was perplexed about how a thief could even get through the security questions. This was bad, Ben thought, someone had all his information. He tried to review the way his information was vulnerable; only one weak link came to mind, Sandy. Was she dumb enough to give his information out? The answer echoed back, "Yes." He knew confronting Sandy was not going to be pretty. He caught Sandy running out the door to go shopping. He knew this was terrible timing. It was comparable to keeping a hungry dog from a bone, but he jumped in without a life vest.

"Babe, before you go I need you for two minutes," he said.

"What is it? I have to go," she replied

"Have you answered any e-mails or spoken to someone on the phone about my credit card information?" Ben queried.

"What is that supposed to mean?" she sniped.

"Someone has gotten my credit card information," he told her.

"Oh sure," she said, "so you think it's my fault."

"That is not what I said."

"No, you're implying it, and I resent it," Sandy said.

"I'm just trying to figure out how they got my information," he said.

"Don't strain your brain. I'm going shopping," Sandy added. Sandy stormed out the door, and he heard the car tires squeal as she left the driveway.

"Oh well," he muttered.

Lucy looked up at him to acknowledge the statement. "I guess it's a dog's world, just us swimming against the tide again."

"C'mon girls, let's go for a walk," Ben said as Lucy and Melanie pranced to the door.

He connected their leashes, and they were off. They walked around the block, and he passed his favorite neighbor's castle. It was cold and dark as usual. Ben kept his eyes on the door, expecting him or his dog to attack them. They passed without incident; he was hoping the dogs would pee on his lawn. They were both too much a lady to be petty. Ben dropped the dogs at home and headed to the police station to report the credit card theft.

Chapter 34

The police station was quiet; Ben rang the bell in the lobby. Marla, the chief's secretary, greeted him.

"Hi Ben," she said. "What brings you here?"

He told her the story of his credit cards. She asked Ben to wait, and she would get someone to take his report. When she returned she informed him, "The chief's the only one here," Marla said. "He said he'll be right out."

The chief popped his head around the corner, "Come on, Ben, I'll take the report in my office," he said.

Ben walked behind him into a comfortable office.

"Hello, chief, thanks for seeing me," Ben said.

Chief Abraham was in his early forties. His uniform was impeccable as usual; Ben often wondered how he kept it wrinkle free through the course of the day. He was willing to bet but never had the guts to ask if he had a steamer or perhaps and ironing board somewhere in his office. Ben gave a furtive glance around, no irons. Even his office was impeccably neat. The chief was well built with a short-cropped military-style haircut. He was pleasant and had a low-key professional mannerism. Ben served a term on the town council and had the pleasure of confirming his nomination for Chief of Police. He was well qualified and a Vietnam veteran. He ran a tight ship with some of the best officers in the state. Over the ensuing years, Ben developed a cordial relationship with the chief that bordered on a genuine friendship. He had the utmost respect for him. Ben felt pride and a sense of mutual respect whenever he had interactions with the chief or his department.

"Have a seat and tell me what brings you here," the chief said.

Ben sat down and proceeded to tell the chief about his problems with the credit cards. Chief Abraham listened intently, writing down the information he needed. He continued to advise Ben of the commonality of this type of crime in the last couple of years. He instructed Ben on how to contact his credit bureaus and put a hold on all transactions in his name. He gave him a pamphlet outlining the common ways your identity is stolen and the steps one can take to minimize the chance of becoming a victim. Ben felt better after seeing him. Identity theft was becoming an all too common crime. Ben was not alone as a victim. The chief informed him that he would not be held liable for the theft and instructed him to request replacement cards with new numbers.

Ben went home and snuggled on the couch with Lucy and Melanie and watched the news. He reflected on how his information could have been stolen. The TV news droned on about one crime after another; it proved terrible things happened every day. Ben realized he would get over this credit mess. He sat with Lucy laying her head on his lap and Melanie slapping him with her paw demanding a belly rub. Ben was content with his two mutts; they always made him feel needed and loved.

Chapter 35

Sandy returned early in the evening and continued to give Ben the cold shoulder. Ben wanted to confront her; he felt he did nothing to deserve her silence and being ignored. As usual, Ben held his tongue and just gave her some room.

Several days passed and Sandy started talking to Ben again. Ben was still upset Sandy that did not help him with Lucy. He ignored her failings as he had always done. Ben ordered new credit cards and informed Sandy the new credit cards would be here shortly so she could give his checkbook a rest. She was pleased, Sandy hated writing checks. Why write when she could swipe Ben's money away? She was in such a good mood Ben even imagined tonight she may be in the mood for him. Their relationship had started very hot and heavy. Sandy cooled down after she moved in; lately, she was always cool to the concept, but after the credit card questioning she became the Ice Queen. Ben had to walk on eggshells and kissed her butt for the last couple of days. Sandy had deftly turned the events to make herself the victim. He sat with Lucy reading science news when the phone rang.

"Hello," he answered.

"Oh hi, it's the Emerson Animal Hospital. Is this Mr. Grece?" she asked.

"Speaking," Ben replied.

"Mr. Grece, your check for Lucy's treatment was returned for insufficient funds," she said. " I'm so sorry; it's most likely an oversight," he answered. "My girlfriend used my checks for some shopping the other day, and I didn't transfer any additional funds to my checking account. She can spend in overdrive. I should have checked," he added.

"Tell Dr. LoFaro I'll stop by tomorrow with the cash, and I'm very sorry for the mix-up," Ben said apologetically.

"I'll tell him; ask for Lisa when you come tomorrow. The bill is three hundred and fifty dollars and twenty-five dollars for the returned check," she said.

"Sorry for the mix-up. I'll see you tomorrow, goodbye," he closed.

Ben went down to his basement office and booted up the computer because he needed to transfer some funds. There was no telling how much Sandy spent the other day. They barely spoke over the past week. Ben pondered what a lousy deal this woman was; she spent his money, berated him constantly, and barely slept with him. He accepted all of her bad habits and she accepted none of his. After Ben lost his parents in an automobile accident, he felt alone and isolated as an only child without any extended family. He liked the company of a woman, even Sandy, and didn't want to be alone. He loved the occasional attention she would give him. Unfortunately, there was very little attention given of late. Ben wondered if he was the dumb one in this relationship. He recalled his single days, lonely and awkward. He hated the pickup scene, and Sandy was a comfortable relationship for him to maintain. Being so one-sided, it was easy, it was almost nonexistent, he thought. Fortunately for Ben, his attachment to the dogs had filled some of the loneliness and his desire to be needed.

Chapter 36

Ben did not want checks bouncing all over town. He clicked on Internet Explorer and loaded up his National Bank sign on. He typed his username and password and received an error message, "No accounts found." "Damn," he thought. He hated typing; he retyped his information and received the same error. He assumed the site was down as usual. The banking site was frequently down. Ben was emotionally and physically exhausted. He went to bed early, hinting to Sandy to do the same. His coaxing fell on deaf ears. Too tired to resort to begging, Ben assured himself that tomorrow was another day.

Ben woke up early and after a light breakfast and walking the dogs he tried to log into his bank accounts with the same result. He did some office work since he was on the PC, and then threw in a load of laundry. He heard Sandy in the kitchen. He finished some accounts and headed upstairs to say hello just in time to hear the front door close. Sandy was off without so much as a good morning.

After lunch, he tried the bank again with the same message, "Account Closed." Ben needed to drop off some dry cleaning, so he decided he would just pass by the bank and make the transfer. Ben was concerned Sandy was still writing checks on the account, and he wanted to minimize the chances of others bouncing.

He arrived at the bank and waited for a bank officer to be available. Ben sat in their uncomfortable utilitarian chair and watched the flurry of activity as the tellers tended to the bank's business. The bank attendant called him to his desk with a broad smile. Ben sat down and explained to the attendant that he needed to transfer some funds from his savings account to the checking account. He gave him his account numbers as the bank official typed in his information.

"I'm sorry, sir, can you give me the number again?" he asked.

Ben repeated the account numbers.

"Huh," the banker said, "Sorry, can you please punch in your social on the keypad. I'm having trouble getting your account in the system."

He punched in his social and the banker clicked and typed away on his PC.

"Is the system down for you also?" Ben asked.

"No, sir, the system is responding; it's indicating you closed these accounts three days ago," he said.

"I haven't done any banking for over a week, are you sure you're looking at the right accounts?" Ben said, concerned.

"Can you type your social again and give me your date of birth?" the banker asked.

Ben typed his social security number again and gave him his date of birth.

"The system is still telling me those accounts are closed." He reviewed Ben's personal information and was sure he had the correct accounts.

"It cannot be right; I have two active accounts with the bank," Ben stressed to the banker.

The banker rose and said, "Let me get the manager to review your accounts; I'll be right back."

He waited fifteen minutes as he watched the manager and the banker discuss his case as they peered at the flashing screens before them. The manager went into a backdoor by the tellers, and the banker returned to him.

"Sorry for the delay, sir, there seems to be a problem with those accounts. The manager is pulling the records now."

"What kind of problem? I have over one hundred eighty thousand in my savings account," Ben said, his voice rising.

"Please, sir, the manager is checking. I'm sure he'll clarify any problems." The manager returned with a detached business demeanor,

"Mr. Grece, our record indicates you closed those accounts three days ago." He had some bond paper in his outstretched hand.

"These are the closing statements and the transfer orders we received," he said.

"Closing statements…are you joking? I didn't close the accounts, I want a full accounting of my money," Ben added in an upset tone.

Ben started to sweat. He felt the perspiration roll down his back as his pulse quickened.

"You need to straighten this mess out. I expect to know where you sent my money, NOW," Ben added as he stood up to make his point.

"Please, Mr. Grece, sit down and please lower your voice," the manager asked as bank customers began to take notice of the commotion. "I'll put an immediate trace on your account, but I can assure you the request was authenticated by our system before any transaction was processed," he said.

"How can you authenticate a transaction I didn't initiate? I want to know how something like this could happen. You let someone take my money?" Ben said in a strained voice. He started to shake, his mouth turned to cotton as he thought over his dilemma. "First my credit cards, and now you jokers don't know where my savings are?

"This is insane, please call for a police officer; I want to file a complaint," he said in a shaky voice. He needed a drink of water as his mouth turned to paste and he had difficulty forming his words.

"Mr. Grece, I'll run a full trace on the transfer and authentication. I'm sure there's an explanation," the manager said. "We will have the full record by morning, and if there are any irregularities, we'll call the authorities."

"You do that, and I'll stop at the police department and file a complaint today. I hope it's just a mistake, and you didn't release my money to a thief," he replied. "I'll be back tomorrow, expect me," Ben added.

He stormed out and headed back to the police station.

Chapter 37

B en found himself back, in the chief's office.

"Hi Ben, how'd things go with the credit bureaus?" the chief asked.

He proceeded to update the chief about his credit cards and informed him about the problem at the bank. The chief told Ben it was not common for identity thieves to hit both credit cards and bank accounts but there had been cases of it happening. The chief explained, "It's a matter of how much data the thieves were able to capture." The chief suspected it was a breach in Ben's computer security.

Chief Abraham filled out a complete report and informed Ben the county's Cybercrime Bureau would be calling him.

"They'll need complete access to your computer," he informed Ben.

"They're welcome to stay in my guest room if it helps them recover my funds and catch the thieves," he replied.

"Expect to hear from me tomorrow. I'll ask for priority response considering the amount of money involved," the chief said.

Ben thanked him and headed for home.

Chapter 38

Ben opened the front door, and there were Lucy and Melanie. His girls were always the first to say hello and the last to say goodbye. Happy, sad, indifferent, depressed, forlorn, desperate didn't matter to them. When he looked into those sparkling eyes, they could melt any mood he brought home. Their greetings made his spirits soar and always gave him hope. "No, the rescue gave me Hope, my Lucy," he thought.

"Do you want to go for a walk, girls?" he asked his dogs. Lucy and Melanie pranced to the door and looked up in agreement. He enjoyed their walks. It gave him time to reflect on and forget the problems of daily life. He grabbed the leashes and off they went. He was approaching the mc-mansion around the block and to his surprise the guy he had the fight with was out checking his mailbox. Ben was glad his dog was not with him. He was again in his tight black jeans, black t-shirt, and sockless boat shoes. Ben wondered if he had a closet full of only black apparel or maybe he was wearing the same clothes from the other day. Ben realized he should not have hit him, nothing justifies violence. Ben called to him.

"Hello," as Vic turned and glared at him.

"I'm sorry about the other day; I don't know what came over me. I hope we can put the incident behind us?" Ben asked.

"Sorry, it's too late to be sorry," he answered. "No, I take it back; I'll make you very, very sorry," he added.

"I'm sorry you feel that way. I'm truly sorry," Ben said, earnestly.

Ben was sincere in his apology, he felt terrible that Vic would not accept his apology. Vic continued to give his veiled threats. Ben had tried; he did not know what else to say.

Vic turned and walked into his house. He could not believe Ben had tried to apologize. He despised the stupid look Ben had on his face and recalled how Max had messed his dog up good. He was going to enjoy his assignment from Manuel. Vic's plan to ruin Ben's life was progressing well, and he was so close to getting into his work account. Vic saw the potential to set him up for fraud. Vic visualized Ben in jail with no resources; it was perfect. When Sergio informed Manuel of the revised plan, Manuel was pleased. If Vic is successful sending Ben to prison for theft, Manuel would make sure he was a victim of a jailhouse brawl. If the stars aligned, per-haps Ben would be sent to Manuel's prison and he would handle his final revenge himself.

Chapter 39

Vic was still stewing over being punched and not answering it back. Vic wanted Ben to pay for hitting him the other day. Financial ruin was just not satisfying enough to Vic. He needed to wipe the dumb smile off his face, so he called Sergio. His brother served as Vic's intermediary. He used him to deal with his contacts, collecting his percentages and, when needed, enforcing the rules. The cell rang on the other end, and Sergio answered.

"Hey," he said.

"Sergio, I have a small job for you," Vic replied.

Vic gave him the address of Ben Grece.

"I want you to beat the smile off his face, make sure he doesn't forget someone doesn't like him for some time to come," Vic added.

"No problem, I'll pay him a little visit tonight," Sergio closed hanging up.

Ben and the dogs continued along. They saw Lolita across the street on her lawn. Lolita was a white, long hair, Great Pyrenees. She was a giant snowball and had a personality to match. She and

Lucy were great sniff buddies. They made an odd couple, a thirty-pound black spaniel mix and a one hundred twenty-pound white polar bear. She was a gentle giant with Lucy. As Lucy and Melanie greeted Lolita, her owner came out.

"Hello, Ben," he said.

"Hi, Mike, how have you been?" Ben chimed back.

"Pretty good and you?" he replied.

"What's up with your neighbor in the castle across the street?" Ben asked. Ben told Mike about the incident with Lucy and his dog. He recounted the story of how he had to punch the dog's owner when Ben thought Vic was going to attack him.

Mike informed him, "He's a real prick; his dog attacked Lolita two months ago and bit a piece of Lolita's nose off. Both dog and owner are nasty, miserable beings."

"That little dog attacked Lolita and lived to bark about it?" Ben laughed.

"Yes, and Lolita is terrified of him now. My wife calls his dog "Jaws." He has attacked several dogs in the neighborhood and the mailman. His owner seems to enjoy when it happens," he said.

"What does the guy do?" Ben asked.

"Rumor is he owns some type of computer company. He doesn't talk to anyone in the neighborhood, in fact, most of us won't talk to him; he's not a friendly sort," he added.

"Too bad. I tried to apologize to him, but he just blew me off. I guess I would hold a grudge if someone punched me," Ben said.

"He deserved a good punch. I, for one, am glad you hit him," Mike said.

"Oh well, I tried," Ben added as he continued on their walk.

Chapter 40

When they arrived home, Sandy was back. Ben told her about his bank accounts being hacked and how the police and the bank were tracing his money.

"What am I going to do? You have no credit cards and now no money," she said.

"What are you going to do? We're talking about my entire savings, perhaps you can try to get a job to help out a little until I get this mess straightened out," Ben said.

"Yeah right, I would sooner go back and makeup with my dad than go and get a job," she said. "You better get it straightened out soon," she threatened.

"The police say it may take some time to recover the money, so until payday we better tighten our belts," he said.

"Tighten my belt, are you joking?" she said. "We have our trip to Aruba booked for next week, you need to have this fixed before then," she said.

"Thanks for reminding me; I'll cancel the hotel and airlines before it's too late. I have some serious financial setbacks to deal with. Aruba is out."

"Yes. You do have some serious problems. The word is you, not I. I still have my savings and I'm going to Aruba with or without you," she said in an obstinate tone, "and come to think of it, I'm going out to dinner tonight. It's a shame you can't afford to come, and I doubt if I'll be back tonight," she said as she stormed out the door and drove off in Ben's car. He sat with Lucy and Melanie, amazed how she turned the entire conversation to herself. He turned on the TV.

"Well, girls, it's just you and me again with leftovers and TV. At least you two are a cheap date," he chuckled to himself.

Ben sat contemplating his relationship with Sandy. He knew she could be quite difficult. Sandy was a victim of her upbringing; the very traits her parents do not like are the same ones they produced. Despite all her selfish needs, there were moments when Ben could still glimpse the person he first met. Ben was her facilitator. He desperately tried not to be, but he could not bring himself to be a harder person. He lived for the occasional caring moment she would share with him. Up to now, it had been enough for him to continue their lopsided relationship. Since Ben adopted Lucy and Melanie, their relationship bothered him even less. His dogs gave him a sense of being loved. Ben knew he was substituting his dogs' attention for human companionship. In his opinion, it was a good substitute. Love from whatever the source is what we crave in our lives. "If an animal is a substitute for a sense of belonging, of being loved, so be it," he thought. A dog's love is unconditional.

Ben stared at Lucy, thinking what a beautiful dog she had grown into. From a scrawny rat-tailed pup, she turned from the ugly duckling into a swan. Her fur grew in as she matured; her ears grew a curl of hair reminiscent of cocker spaniel's ears. Her body fur was wavy and soft, hanging down long enough to bounce as she walked or ran. Her legs had the wavy curl of a cocker spaniel's except for the front of her lower paws which remained short. Her tail grew a beautiful mane of hair tapering in length to the tip. She kept her tail held straight out and proud with a never tiring wag. She stood eighteen inches ground to shoulder. A fit thirty pounds, she was slender and muscular, a tireless runner and swimmer outside and a snuggler in. She was empathetic and friendly to all, both human and dog. She was a relentless hunter who enjoyed chasing small critters but would not capture or harm them. Wherever they went, people would ask what kind of a dog she was or comment on how beautiful she was. Who could blame them? She was a beauty with those piercing eyes, so how could they resist?

Chapter 41

Ben and the dogs finished supper and watched TV for a couple of hours. He took Lucy and Melanie out, and they went to bed. Lucy curled on her dog bed, and he covered her with her blanket. Melanie flopped down on the far side of his bed on the hardwood. Ben was exhausted from the day's events and barely remembered his head hitting the pillow.

He woke to the sound of Lucy growling. The room was dark with just a sliver of moonlight projecting through the closed blinds onto the far wall. Ben could make out the silhouette of Lucy looking towards the door. "What's the matter, girl, did you have a bad dream?" he asked. As the words left his mouth, a dark figure came through the bedroom door. Lucy met him in the doorway with a growl and a partial bark as the apparition viciously kicked at his girl. The intruder was slim and well-built from his silhouette. He was holding something long and thin in his left hand. It was too dark to make out his features. Lucy let out a yelp as she jumped on the bed and moved behind Ben. Ben was extricating himself from the covers, and as his feet hit the ground, the first blow hit him across the face. Something hard and cold struck him with enough force to knock Ben back onto the bed. Electric sparks flashed in his eyes. Lucy was behind Ben and started barking.

He rolled to get back up from the bed, but the attacker grabbed his foot and yanked him out of bed. Ben so quickly that his shoulder and head hit the hardwood floor with all the force of his weight. Ben was dazed, unsure of what was happening or even where he was for a moment. His only thought was to tell himself to "get up, get up, and cover-up." Ben struggled to his feet as several more blows made contact with his hands as he covered his head. The intruder was swinging a pipe or perhaps a tire iron. Each blow stung and sent shooting pain into Ben's limbs.

Ben rushed at his attacker, tackling him at the waist. He pushed the assailant back through the bedroom door slamming him against the bedroom door frame, jarring both himself and the attacker. Holding his attacker's torso tightly, the blows lessened, he couldn't get a full swing with Ben hugging his waist. Ben was propelled into the hall and lifted off his feet. All he could hear was the panicked barking of Lucy and the ringing in his ears from the blows. Ben held on for dear life, but as he was slammed against the wall, Ben felt his grip loosen as a wave of pain shot through his spine. He was flipped, thrown like a rag doll down the hall steps. Ben hit the hardwood floor at the bottom of the stairs with a thud and pain racked his body as flashes shot in the back of his eyes. Ben was confused and not sure where he had landed. There was still the dull drone of Lucy's bark and a ringing in his ears. He looked up and saw his attacker's blurry face as he calmly walked down the steps. "Who was this and what did he want?" he thought.

"Take what you want," Ben muttered. "Please stop, I'm hurt."

His words still echoed in his ears as Ben felt a foot pound into his abdomen. His stomach retched from the sharp pain it produced. Ben balled up trying to protect his vital organs. There were several sharper kicks before the attacker turned and left. He uttered something as he walked away. Ben thought he heard, "How you like it now?" but he was not sure, his ears were ringing loudly, and Lucy was furiously barking at the top of the steps.

He watched his assailant disappear down the basement steps and out the door. Ben lay beaten and bleeding, wondering what had just happened. He felt the gastric juices in the back of his throat as his stomach balked at the thought of retaining the vile fluid one second longer. He swallowed, and his guts countered with painful cramping and burning in the back of his gullet that made him think perhaps he should just let it come up.

Chapter 42

Ben felt a warm, gentle tongue lick his bloody face. His eyes were blurry perhaps from the blood, maybe it was a concussion; he tried not to overthink his predicament. Lucy, his princess of a mutt, lay down beside him and washed the blood from his face. His baby wanted to comfort him, snuggling her body against his, caressing him with her mothering tongue. At least someone still loved him; it takes a dog to give unconditional love even at your worst moment. Ben carefully evaluated his wounds. His body was a combination of aches and pains. Ben's left arm was free, and he slowly moved it over his convulsing gut, probing his tender belly. It was painful; he expected the pain considering his opponents boot found his soft underbelly several times after he hit the ground. It was still soft; Ben was relieved, hoping he had no internal bleeding. A lacerated liver from a swift kick could quickly end a life.

Lucy continued to wash Ben's face, and his eyesight started to clear. He moved his legs, sore but all parts moved. He took a mental inventory. "No broken bones, I guess my back wasn't broken; I think my spinal cord is intact, everything is moving and painful." Neurons, still firing, found their way from his brain to his legs. Ben's right shoulder and arm apparently did not do as well. Pain shot from his shoulder into the bicep, and it rebelled at being moved. He gingerly tucked his right arm against his body and tried to roll onto his left side. Keeping the right arm tucked against his body, he propped himself up on his left arm. His gut convulsed; Ben again felt the acidic bite of stomach contents rushing into the back of his throat. He swallowed hard and fought back the vomit. His right shoulder screamed, his ribs and belly ached. Ben broke out into a sweat with the anxiety and pain. He was thinking something must be broken or he may be bleeding internally. He felt his heart beating in his ears, his eyes started to blur, and the room went into a horrible spin.

Ben woke to his Lucy's gentle washing. He went back through the entire painful process again in an attempt to sit. Ben propped himself up against the side of the couch and felt queasy and light-headed, hoping he would not black out again. Ben again began to assess his many injuries again, carefully moving each joint, running through a mental checklist, movement yes, pain yes, any deformity or swelling, any funky grating or sounds? As he inventoried his body, Ben saw his princess's eyes piercing his pain. Her adoring brown eyes, those beautifully eyes felt Ben's pain. Her eyes asked how she could help him, her face full of concern.

Ben reflected on this petite black mutt. Can an animal feel compassion or empathy? God, Ben knew Lucy could. She is a person reborn as a dog. This thirty-pound black mutt understood Ben. She accepted his shortfalls. She was never judgmental or condescending. Unlike Sandy, his so-called girlfriend, who walked out on him last night as his comfortable life spiraled out of control. Ben thought, "If she were here, she would be standing over me telling me what a screw-up I was and that I deserved everything that was happening." He felt lucky she had walked out on him; at least he no longer had to hear her crap. Lucy didn't badger Ben unless she wanted to go out for a hike or to play; she would never tell him how he messed up, she would just stare at him with those adorable eyes asking permission to wash his face some more and mother his hurt away.

Chapter 43

Ben didn't think he was a bad person deserving of such calamity. Ben was an investment banker with National Bank in Hackensack, New Jersey. He ran a substantial small-cap fund and had profited investors and his institution. He was a volunteer EMS. Ben always had a desire to help people, but he did not think he had the "stuff" to be in the medical field. Eleven years ago the town ambulance squad was in need of members. The captain of the ambulance squad did business with his bank and convinced Ben to volunteer. It was an intensive and fun course. He spent two nights a week and some weekends over six months and was certified as an EMT. Ben was transformed from someone who barely could put on a Band-Aid into a functional emergency responder. That was eleven years ago, and he had enjoyed helping the sick and injured ever since.

Ben recalled his first ambulance call. It was two in the morning on a Friday. His crew chief, the medic in charge, was a nurse, paramedic, EMT and had over twenty years' experience. Who better to learn from? He assumed she had seen it all. They were called to a motor vehicle rollover. As they approached the accident scene from down the road, Ben's heart raced with each wail of the siren. Ahead was the largest collection of fire engines and police cars Ben had ever seen. Each vehicle appeared to have a hundred flashing lights. His mouth went dry, and he felt the nervous sweat running down his back. He felt comforted only by the fact he was riding with one of the town's veteran medics. In the center of the flashing lights was an overturned car with its roof partially crushed, broken glass was scattered along the road, and a body was hanging lifelessly upside down, suspended by a seat belt. Ben's crew chief looked the scene over and commented, "Holy crap."

"Holy crap?" Ben repeated. "What do you mean holy crap? Don't you see this all the time?" he said as his pulse quickened and his head grew lighter.

"No, this looks bad," she replied back.

They pulled up to the car, and he was in full panic. He prepared himself to see his first dead person. All this and on his first call. He grabbed the jump bag with supplies and was told by the fire chief the car was safe and someone needed to check if the victim was still alive. Ben's crew chief instructed him to reach in and feel for a carotid pulse on the driver, who was hanging limply upside down in the car. His hand shook as he reached a gloved hand to his neck. When Ben's hand touched his neck, the man's eyes popped open as he exclaimed, "It's my birthday," in a slurred intoxicated voice. Ben nearly wet himself as a flood of relief poured over his being. The victim was very much alive. It was an intoxicated driver returning from his birthday bash. After the fire department cut him out of the car, he only had minor cuts and bruises. He just needed somewhere to sleep it off. Unfortunately for them, he chose his upside-down vehicle. Ben smiled to himself as the memory flashed through his mind. His mind continued to wander in a semi-conscious dreamlike state.

Ben reflected on how he was recently honored for heroism by the ambulance squad and the town. He was driving home from work on a beautiful Saturday afternoon. The light in the center of the town was red. Ben stopped and waited for the green. On the right was a strip of stores. There was the local hardware store, florist, deli, and others. The train station was to the left, and the adjacent tracks were separated from the road by an aluminum fence. Several commuters were waiting for a train home. Ben watched a Chrysler PT Cruiser drive through the stations parking lot across the platform and onto the train tracks. He sat in his car thinking how stupid a person could be. Then the car fell off the edge of the eighteen-inch platform and was stuck. He watched the woman in the car and the people on the platform. Ben remembered thinking this would be a wrong time for a train to come. No sooner did the thought pass when the gates of the train crossing started ringing and lowering. He recounted the story of an old woman whose car stalled on the tracks a decade ago. Bystanders begged her to get out of the vehicle when the gates lowered. The woman kept trying to start the car. The train hit her car, and she died. Ben did not want to witness a similar event. He jumped from his car screaming and waving his arms for her to get out of the car. She sat and spun the wheels, her vehicle now lodged firmly on the tracks and platform. Someone had to get her out of the car. Without thinking, he found himself running around the gate towards the car, the train whistle now steady. He tore open her door begging her to get out.

"Get out! You'll die in this car," Ben yelled to her.

"No, get away, my car is new," she answered with the tires spinning as she raced the engine.

The train whistle grew ever louder, the sound vibrating in Ben's ears. The train's brakes squealed down the tracks, and it bore down on her car. He dared not look back; the train would be on them soon.

"You have to get out now," he said as he grabbed her arm and waistband. Ben pulled as hard as he could and yanked her out of the driver's seat. She landed on her feet and pushed him back towards the car and train tracks. The train's whistle continued to bear down, Ben pushed back knocking her off her feet. He again grabbed her wrist and waistband and dragged her behind the side of the train station just as the train passed slamming into her car. Ben's heart beat wildly, and he could barely catch his breath as the car was pushed down the tracks and under the locomotive. Ben let the woman go, and still screaming, she ran down the platform after her car.

Ben was lifted into town-wide legendary status for saving the women. Stories made the local papers. Friends and neighbors congratulated him. He was glad they were both alive to tell the story. Ben was given awards by the town, the ambulance squad, fire and the police. Ben was already known to many from his term as a town councilman and his EMT work. This incident brought his recognition to a new height. He recounted what a fantastic experience it was and admitted to himself he was never more scared in his life.

His dog's movement broke Ben's reminiscences, returning him back to the pain.

Chapter 44

Lucy moved closer to Ben and pressed her soft body against him, keeping him from listing to the injured side as he assessed the damage. She tried to clean some blood from his hair as he told her, "Enough, girl." This spaniel mix was the only good he could find in his life at this moment. She made him want to stay conscious. If love is unconditional, Lucy is love. In the last couple of weeks, his dogs remained the only reason he kept his life together. Lucy is his Prozac, flushing away the fears and anxiety of life, keeping him grounded in the face of his out of control circumstances. She helped him to cope. He reflected on how his spoiled brat of a girlfriend was responsible for his having Lucy.

Four years ago Sandy decided they needed to get a dog. "Great, a dog," Ben thought as if he didn't have his hands full with Sandy. She was not the neatest of persons. Ben was proud of his modest home in the burbs. It was neat and clean with new furnishings. He often had to clean up behind Sandy. Cleaning up behind a dog and dealing with the chewing and training was not appealing to him. He would need a full-time live-in to keep up with Sandy and a dog.

Sandy obsessed over what breed to get. She wondered what type of dog would look good with them. Ben had visions of her carrying a hairless Chihuahua in her Gucci bag feeding it scraps at La Chic, his favorite restaurant, right before the maître de asked them to leave, "Pardon, monsieur, but pets are not allowed, I must ask you to take the animal out."

He imagined Sandy throwing a fit of anger that their favorite restaurant would dare rebuff her designer dog. Sandy searched breeders and pedigrees; Ben took to Petfinder to find a rescue. He knew Sandy would not give up on her dog; he surrendered to the fact that he was going to end up with a dog. Ben felt if he was to have a dog he might as well help a homeless one. The website allowed you to search by the breed of dog you wanted. The search could be narrowed by age, baby, young, adult or senior. You could search by location, distance from you or gender, male or female. Ben was fascinated and saddened. There were so many lost friends, soul mates, and companions. A sea of lost animals, looking for someone to love them. If we are an intelligent species then how could we cast aside so many of the animals we domesticated? There were so many to choose from, each adorable dog, one by one, was shot down by Sandy.

"That dog is too old."

"No way, I wouldn't be caught dead with that beast."

"That one is hideous."

She told Ben, "These dogs are the dregs of the dog world, they should be destroyed."

"I thought you were a compassionate person," Ben said.

"Of course I am," she replied. "Who is more compassionate than me?"

"Well, if you're so kind then why not adopt a rescue dog?" he said.

"Well maybe I'll do it," she added. "I have much better taste than the losers you have been showing me."

Ben told her, "Why don't you look on the site yourself and find a dog?"

"Maybe I will," she snapped back. "You obviously have no taste in dogs."

"Great," he said, "knock yourself out."

Chapter 45

With a gauntlet thrown, Sandy was determined to prove Ben wrong again; she went to work on Petfinder to show Ben she could find a dog worthy of her affection. She had to prove she could rescue a dog since she was a kind and compassionate person. It took her just two hours to find such a dog worthy.

"Look at this cutie," she said. "This is the dog I want," she added.

Ben looked at two pups in a basket on the site; one was a white and tan female with spaniel ears that looked like a Brittany spaniel, the other a black female, so black you only saw her deep brown eyes. Those eyes could stare through you from a web page. Those deep, soulful eyes.

"God, look at the eyes on that pup," Ben said.

"Isn't she beautiful? She looks like a pedigree Brittany," Sandy said.

"I was referring to the black pup," he said.

"Are you kidding me? That black rat? The black dog looks horrible," she quipped.

Ben just dropped the conversation. She made him fill out the adoption application for the beige pup in the basket.

"The beige one is named Faith, what an adorable name," she said.

"So the black one is Hope?" he replied.

"Yeah, the black rat is hopeless," she added.

Together they filled out the fifteen-page application he thought was ridiculous considering these were homeless mutts. He believed it may be easier to buy her a hairless pocket dog and have done with it. Ben kept thinking about those eyes; the dog had such soulful eyes.

Sandy was obsessed with getting her Brittany. They did not hear anything after the application was submitted. Sandy began to e-mail the rescue daily. She complained to Ben that they received no replies from the rescue and demanded Ben drive to the address on the web site and get the dog. Ben was way too busy to go on a wild dog chase and thankfully the rescue finally responded to her inquiries. The dogs, two sisters, were held over in the Carolinas due to health issues. They were being boarded at a veterinarian until he could clear them to travel. The rescue assured the couple they were being considered for the dog, pending a home inspection. She would contact them when the dog was healthy enough to travel.

Chapter 46

Sandy proceeded to drive Ben crazy, complaining about the rescue, the vet, the sick dog.

"Maybe we should forget the whole thing," she insisted.

"Who knows what diseases the dog will give us," she said.

"Dogs don't spread disease to humans," Ben answered. "Are you ready to give up already?"

"No," she replied.

"No, what?" Ben asked

"No, I'm not giving up, "she added.

Ben questioned himself as to why he was defending getting a dog. He thought perhaps he should let Sandy forget the whole thing.

Sandy kept e-mailing the rescue daily, and approximately a month later they received a response. A representative of the rescue would be coming to the house to inspect it. They set a date, and Sandy drove Ben nuts waiting for the inspection. She bought a dog bed, squeaky toys, treats, food and water dishes, and opined about the possibility of not passing inspection. Ben did his part making sure the yard was escape proof. He owned a modest split-level home in the burbs with a fenced-in yard he thought would be great for a dog. On inspection day they were ready. Ben watched as a white panel van parked in front of the house. When he answered the door, there stood a young woman in her mid-twenties, holding a squirming black pup with a thin rat-like tail. The woman wore a yellow flower print sundress with matching flats. She had an upbeat, perky demeanor and was as adorable as the small pup she held. She introduced herself as Anita. Ben wondered what happened to the Brittany pup Sandy so desired. Before his mouth could say a word the eyes of the puppy gazed into his. Both the pup and Ben were frozen in time for the moment. Ben felt he knew this dog's soul and she knew his. It was at that moment Ben knew they were to be together; soul mates, a family love which transcends our mundane life. An unseen bond formed in a moment, a relationship which could not be broken. He stood there motionlessly staring into the pup's eyes, and it did the same. Ben must have freaked out his guest because she asked him, "Are you alright?"

Startled back to reality, "Yes," Ben replied. "I'm sorry. Come on in," he said.

Sandy deftly inserted herself between Ben and Anita.

"Yes, please come in," she said. "We have everything ready for our little puppy," she added as she noticed the scruffy black bundle in the woman's arms. The young lady introduced herself to Sandy. Ben could see the expression change in Sandy's face as she looked from the pup to the woman and back. He knew this encounter was going to become awkward. Ben moved quickly.

"Anita, let me hold the pup so you and Sandy can tour the house," he injected, "Sandy, please show Anita how we prepared for a puppy."

"What's with the black d….?" Sandy said as Ben interrupted.

"Sandy, show her the yard; dogs need a big yard," he said.

"Wonderful! I would love to see the yard," Anita said. "Exercise and room to run are so important to keep a dog healthy," she added.

Ben herded them out into the yard, keeping the pup tucked against his side; this adorable pup seemed content in his arms.

He waited in the house, Ben and this ratty looking puppy with the soulful eyes. He held her up in one hand and looked into those eyes.

"Who are you?" he asked. The pup just stared back and licked his thumb. "Freaky," he thought, "why did this little ball of fluff evoke such strong feeling in him?" Whatever the reason, Ben decided he was keeping this dog. With that thought, Sandy and Anita returned from the yard. The inspection distracted Sandy enough to forget Ben's little black prize. When she saw him holding the black pup, Sandy's sneer returned.

"What's with the black dog?" she asked Anita.

"Oh, this is Hope, isn't she adorable?" Anita said.

"Where's the Brittany spaniel? I thought you'd be bringing her," Sandy replied.

"Oh, you mean Faith; she is a spaniel mix, not a Brittany. She's still in the Carolinas. She's still too sick to travel, so I brought her sister. She has such a gentle temperament," Anita added.

"It looks like there's still something wrong with the dog. Just look at it, my God are you trying to give us a disease?" Sandy quipped.

"Oh no, she is in good health, she even has had her first series of shots," Anita said. Before Sandy could continue, Ben interjected, "She appears fine to me; we'll be glad to adopt her."

"Are you kidding? You want us to keep that thing?" Sandy snapped.

He said, "We can keep her while the other dog gets better, you know, like a foster parent."

"I don't think so," Sandy said.

"I see no problems with your house," Anita added, "but I don't want you to take an animal you don't want."

"No, we want to foster this dog at least until her sister is available; it's no problem. Sandy and I always wanted to foster dogs," Ben said.

"We never…" Ben interrupted Sandy as he slowly herded Anita towards the door.

"No, no, it will be fine, we will take good care of her; call us when her sister is better," he said as he closed the front door.

"But….but," Ben heard Anita saying as the door clicked shut.

"Don't worry! We'll take good care of her. Call us," he yelled through the door.

"Have you lost your mind?" Sandy screeched, "And what was all the crap about us always wanting to foster dogs?"

"I…"

She interrupted him saying, "Seriously, look at the rat you're holding; you better get that diseased animal out of this house."

Ben stopped listening; the only animal going out of his house would be Sandy if he had to choose. He took his precious cargo and headed to show her the nice new bed Sandy bought for her.

"Look, baby, this is your new home. We got you a comfy bed," Ben told the pup.

"You're not putting the dog on the new bed; it's not for her," Sandy said.

"Let it go, Sandy, you're really starting to piss me off. The dog is staying so get used to it," he stated.

"When the Brittany comes, the other one goes," Sandy said.

"Whatever," Ben said, "but for now get used to her. I like her."

Ben watched as the puppy snuggled into the soft dog bed and watched as the beautiful brown eyes grew heavier and heavier until the pups breathing fell into a smooth, steady rhythm. He just lay on the floor next to her watching her sleep, thinking what great fate this was: Anita brought the black pup not the beige one. Hope, she brought him hope, but as far as a dog's name, that he was not so sure.

"Well, little girl, what should we call you?" Ben whispered.

He lay there thinking, and he could hear the rumblings of discontent, known as Sandy, in the other room. She sounded miserable, banging pots and pans and slamming cabinets closed as she fixed herself lunch. All he could think was, at this moment, he was happy; happy with this little pup he fell in love with at first sight. Sandy turned on the TV and

Ben heard the theme song for *I Love Lucy*. "Lucy, yes, I love Lucy," he concluded from the song.

"Well girl, I think it fits. Lucy, I love you," he whispered as Lucy looked up and gave a small yawn. Ben thought he was genuinely nuts to feel so attached to this little dog.

Chapter 47

B en sat against the couch looking at Lucy. He smiled to himself in spite of the pain as he recounted their first meeting. Lucy quickly became a part of his life; her sister Faith never materialized. After Faith was cleared to travel, Anita found a family in Connecticut who adopted her. Anita did call the following day about Lucy and Ben told her everything was going great and they decided to keep the black pup. Anita tried to convince him they were only fostering and once she found a home, they would have to give the dog up. He informed her they changed their minds and both fell in love with Lucy and would keep her. Ben would hear no different. Anita was hesitant to accept his offer to adopt the dog. Ben argued his case, and the frustrated Anita agreed to allow them to adopt Lucy. Ben was given the impression that Anita feared he was emotionally unbalanced. Ben believed it was the reason she did not pursue getting Lucy back. He sent her the adoption fee and an incredibly generous donation. He hoped it was large enough that the rescue would not want to refuse it and give it back. He recalled the look on Anita's face as he nudged her out of his house and closed the door. It was priceless, and if she didn't call the police that day, then he guessed he won.

Anita called again two months later to tell Sandy Lucy's sister was adopted by another family, and the only reason she called was that Sandy was still e-mailing the rescue every day to inquire about Faith. It was approximately six months before Sandy stopped reminding Ben how he screwed up her adoption because of his black rat. In the meantime, Lucy was growing up. She was as smart as a whip. She had one accident on her second day with them and not one since. She held her business in and waited at the door for Ben to walk her. On days when he was at work, Sandy would ignore her for hours. Sandy hoped she would mess the house as an excuse to remind Ben what a bad dog he had chosen. Lucy would not give her the satisfaction. Lucy would wait Sandy's ire out until either she took her out or Ben came home.

Lucy quickly became a part of his life and routine. Ben walked her every morning before work, even if he was working from home. He walked her every evening. They had their ritual walk, blocks they liked the most. Ben especially liked to see their dog friends, Libby the shy shepherd mix, Lilly a pugnacious pug, Samantha the bouncing boxer, Kaia the puggle, Teddy and Bella the teddy bear dogs, Spencer the cock-a-poo, Patty and Belle the Australian shepherds and Lolita a gentle Great Pyrenees. Lucy would greet each one with warm enthusiasm. Ben would often talk with their owners if they happened to be out. They loved their daily walks. In the evenings and weekends, Ben could often convince Sandy to tag along. On beautiful days when he worked from home, he often would take a few hours off and take Lucy on a longer hike. He had several favorites ranging from mountain trials at Ramapo Reservation to walks along the base of the Hudson River's towering Palisades Cliffs. Ben was lucky to have been raised in North Bergen County, New Jersey. It is a short ride to New York City and close to some of the most scenic and pet-friendly parks. Lucy kept Ben engaged in his life and healthier as a result.

Chapter 48

Ben remained propped against the couch guarded by his Lucy. The pain prevented him from moving from his current position. Ben was dozing in and out of a fuzzy consciousness. He feared he would not wake up if he fell asleep, so Ben forced himself to remain awake. He sat and watched the sunrise and the world come back to life. Ben was afraid to move in fear of the pain and prayed someone would find him. His cell phone was in his bedroom which now seemed to be a mile away. Lucy sat vigilantly by his side keeping him company. Ben heard the door opening as dread passed through his body. "Is my attacker returning to finish the job?"

Lucy barked her protective bark as Sandy walked through the door. He couldn't remember a time when he was more glad to see Sandy. Her eyes fell on his bloodied figure as she screeched "Oh my God!"

Sandy called 911, and soon the house was filled with police and EMS. The medics checked Ben's vitals and asked him what hurt. Ben replied, "Everything hurts." The blood pressure cuff hurt as it squeezed his sore arm. The pulse oximeter, the device that checks the oxygen in your blood, hurt his finger. Ben's stomach revolted with new regurgitation as it was checked for bleeding. His head pounded, his ears rang, and the hustle and bustle around him seemed dreamlike. It was all surreal until they attempted to move Ben onto the stretcher. At that moment every nerve cell in his brain came alive to experience new places for pain. Ben moaned as they placed him on the waiting stretcher. He heard Sandy say, "Stop being a baby."

He guessed his predicament and pain embarrassed her. Police moved through the house room by room, guns drawn, looking for any remaining intruders. The officer checking the bathroom noticed the shower curtain move. Ben heard the officer yell, "Here!" as he entered the bathroom. He stood with gun pointing into the room as a second offer came behind him for backup.

"The tub, someone is behind the curtain," the first officer stated as the second officer squatted training his gun on the tub.

"Police, come out hands raised," the first officer commanded.

The shower curtain moved slightly, but no one emerged.

"Police, come out now," the officer repeated.

The tension was building in the house as the medics and Sandy retreated out the door and another officer with gun drawn squatted by Ben's side shielding him and eying the transpiring event.

When no one emerged, the first officer signaled with hand motions that he was moving in. The other officer remained crouched with his gun ready. The officer grabbed and quickly drew the curtain back with his gun pointed at the tub. The curtain and rod pulled loose and fell to the tile floor with a metallic clunk. The second officer started laughing when he saw Melanie sitting in the tub shaking and drooling profusely.

"Holy crap, it's a dog," the first officer said, relieved.

Ben had forgotten about Melanie in all the confusion. Melanie had apparently retreated to the tub, her safe haven, during the fight. Sandy informed the officers that Melanie was their other dog. The police were trying to get some of the essential events of the incident as the medics returned and asked Ben for medical and medication history. The words were a confusing mix of phrases, and he only remembered stating his name and date of birth. They thought he may have suffered brain trauma because of his lack of response. Ben did hear the voice of Sandy expressing concern about the blood on the floor and couch.

"Don't you men clean this mess up? The blood will stain and can spread disease," she implored them.

"Spread disease? It's my blood, the blood of the man she occasionally or should I say rarely sleeps with," Ben thought. As they wheeled Ben out the door, he managed to tell Sandy to take care of Lucy and Melanie.

Chapter 49

The emergency room was chaos. They transferred Ben onto a stretcher in a hallway and left him there. He watched as nurses and attendants passed back and forth seeming not to notice him lying in the hall. Ben didn't care; it had been a long night, and he finally could get some sleep. Sleep proved to be elusive though. The glare from the fluorescent light pierced his skull. He lay thinking even the light hurt. He stressed over the extent of his injuries and worried that he might have permanent damage. He was wondering what was happening to his life. If bad things happened in threes, this was the third event. First his credit cards, then the bank accounts and now a prowler. Ben did not know what the prowler might have stolen, the incident was very fuzzy. It seemed to happen so fast. The only clear image he had was Lucy barking at the top of the steps, and the blurred face of his attacker. Ben was just dozing off when he became aware of someone standing next to his stretcher; it was his friend, Chief Abraham.

"Ben, how are you feeling? I heard the call when I was just finishing a meeting with the mayor."

"It's nice to see someone noticed me here; I think they forgot about me," Ben said.

"This isn't just a social call. I was told you couldn't give a statement at your home, so if you're up to it, I'd like a statement from you now. I want to get the person who did this to you," he said.

Ben gave the chief his fuzzy account of the events.

"Was anything taken from my house?" he asked.

"My officers reported a broken lock on the basement door appears to be his entry point, their cursory inspection noted nothing disturbed on your dressers or shelves. There were only the signs of the assault. The only highlight was the dog in the tub! Officer Boland is still telling the story," he said.

"They had Sandy walk through the house, and she reported nothing appeared missing. You'll have to confirm it when you get home," The chief added.

"Nothing was stolen," Ben said in a surprised tone.

"The prowler must not have been expecting anyone home and fled after the assault," he said. "Can you identify him? I can get a sketch artist over here," the chief asked.

"I wish I could. I have a blurry image of him. I'll do the best I can to describe him," Ben said.

The nurse came over and told the chief Ben was due for a CT scan. The chief told Ben when he was discharged to come to the police department if he was up to it or if he was admitted or not able to get there he would send a sketch artist to him. Ben's CT scan was negative, and X-rays showed no broken bones. His diagnosis was a concussion with multiple contusions. The doctor admitted him for observation overnight due to the amount of swelling he had. Everywhere Ben looked was black and blue with some degree of swelling.

Chapter 50

Sandy came to take Ben home in the morning with her cheerful, "You look like crap" hello. On the ride home, she informed him she was going to stay with a "friend" for a few days because his house was a mess.

"Do you believe they left blood everywhere? I told them to clean it up, but they just ignored me," she complained.

"Sandy, I was beaten up badly, I could use some help at home," Ben said sheepishly.

"Oh you'll be fine; you don't need me there, besides I already promised my friend I would be coming for a few days."

"Did you feed and walk Lucy and Melanie?" Ben asked.

"Lucy? I think you care more about the dog than me," she stated.

"No babe, how could you say that," his mouth said as his mind screamed, "You better believe it." His dogs are more compassionate and caring beings than she would ever be! He was getting upset thinking Sandy may not have properly cared for the dogs and was probably heading to her new boyfriend's place. She dropped Ben off at the curb and gave him a blown kiss saying.

"Sorry, you are too grungy for me. I'll be back tomorrow or the day after, so see if you can get the place cleaned up and please take a shower."

"Like I don't shower daily, what a darling I have there," Ben thought.

She drove off with his car. Lucy and Melanie were so excited to see Ben; their greeting dance was only outdone by the wagging of tails. They appeared to be happy, so he guessed Sandy did feed them. He checked their water dish and thankfully there was still some water in it. Lucy seemed to be okay with no signs of lingering injury from being kicked. The two pranced around Ben; they wanted to go for a walk. Ben's aching body refused to consider it. He let them out on the front lawn, and the poor things were busting. He bet Sandy never let the dogs out. They took care of business, and Ben herded them inside and up to the bedroom and went to bed. He called in sick to work for the next two days. Although he frequently worked from home, Ben had no intention of working feeling as he did. He only moved from bed to eat and feed the dogs, let the dogs out on the lawn, and toilet himself. To heck with the front lawn he thought, he would clean it when he felt better. Lucy knew Ben was hurting, she lay on his bed, something she knows is off limits, and gently washed his face until he brushed her away. She and Melanie were his support for his brief convalescence, his reason to get up.

Chapter 51

Vic was diligently working on Ben's stock account. He was able to circumvent the stock funds security. He proceeded to remove eight hundred and fifty thousand dollars from the account. Vic set up an easily traceable offshore account in the name of Ben Grece and deposited one hundred thousand in it. He sent the remaining seven hundred and fifty along a cascade of dummy accounts ultimately into his own pocket. It was a test withdrawal looking for any bugs in the scripts he wrote to override the security. He was nervous about all the security attached to the account. Vic had limited his work to consumer credit cards. They are easily hacked, and the credit companies, as well as the police, have little desire to pursue credit theft. The banking industry writes off millions of dollars of credit theft as the cost of doing business. Consumer theft did not generate the level of outrage a direct robbery would inspire. Most credit theft does not hold the consumer responsible. Banks and debit cards were trickier to hack. They had tighter security checks, and bank account movements were monitored closely and were easier to trace. ATM's are the easier mark since they limited withdrawals to three or four hundred dollars and had the same interest level as credit card theft. Securities accounts are an entirely different animal.

Usually, Vic would not want to tackle something as substantial as National Bank. He decided it was fate, so why look a gift horse in the mouth. Setting up Ben would put him in Manuel's graces and provide a rich reward: the payment from Manuel and all he could steal from Ben. Vic made sure he would have no trouble removing the cash from any significant stock sales he initiated. The transaction went flawlessly. He waited eight hours to confirm the deposit. A runner would withdraw the money, and the last account would be closed. Vic spent some time looking for any traces on his transactions. It appeared all went well. He was ready to move a hundred million along his cascade of accounts ending in thirty separate accounts. He had runners in place, prepared to empty the accounts and move the funds into obscurity. Retirement was a few keystrokes away.

Vic had fallen into a potential windfall of cash when he accepted Manuel Garcia's contract. Ben was the golden goose. Too bad the goose would go to jail where Manuel could do what he wanted with him. Vic re-logged onto the account. His scripts were ready to run, ordering the sales and routing the funds through the cascade of temporary accounts he made. Vic started his symphony of computer programs, it all was moving so beautifully. He slipped on his headphones playing Beethoven's 5th. He was the maestro on the keyboard playing Ben's farewell song.

The sales orders went out when suddenly the account shut him down. Vic's system crashed mid-transaction. As he debugged the crash; someone overrode his access and was sorting through the dummy accounts. This appeared not to be a simple security inquiry; whoever they were, they were burning through his encryptions and moving very fast through the web of dummies.

Vic threw his headphones down; he had to concentrate. He knew he had to self-destruct before his trail was visible. Vic was so close to the biggest payday of his life. National Bank was more advanced than he had anticipated; he hoped it wasn't Homeland Security looking. Vic ran the self-destruct script. The program wiped the system clean. Any trace or trail to him was erased in seconds. Whoever was tracking his activity would find the path had vanished and any hints of the attempt unrecoverable. Vic slammed his hands down on his desk, so close to millions and yet so far, it left Vic with only a consolation prize of seven hundred and fifty thousand dollars. He wondered if the dork Grece was the one responsible for shutting down his plans. Vic doubted Ben had the skills to trace his handiwork. It must have been bank security.

Vic smiled at the thought that Ben would not be able to explain away the offshore account. Vic doubted he would be seeing Ben or his mutts for a long time.

Chapter 52

After two days of rest, Ben was itching to go back to work. Sandy returned as irritable as ever; he was glad his car came back with her. Ben knew he had to make a cameo at the office, so he commandeered his car and was off to work. Ben had been out of the office for two weeks. He frequently worked from home. He was looking forward to stopping in and seeing his dusty office. As the financial officer for National Trust Bank, Ben handled their bond acquisitions and oversaw their small-cap stock fund. He entered the lobby of the impressive Hackensack branch. It was a full-service bank branch with two floors of administrative offices above. The desk receptionist, Nancy, looked surprised to see Ben.

"Good morning," he piped to her.

"Oh, hi, Mr. Grece," she replied. Mr. Grece? He wondered why the formality. She always called him Ben; he had an informal relationship with her. As Ben passed, she nervously dialed the phone and took precautions to muffle her conversation as she spoke. He thought it odd as he entered the elevator. On the third floor, Ben said a few hellos as he headed for his office. Ben had an upscale corner office. It was well appointed with artwork from some local artists he favored, an oak desk and a leather captains and side chairs. He hit the on-button of his PC and opened the blinds to let the warm sunshine in. He was in for less than five minutes; the computer didn't even have time to boot, before the bank president walked in with Frank, the head of security. Mark Walker, the bank president, and regional director hired Ben directly from college twenty-one years ago. Ben was employed as a financial assistant for his predecessor, Norman Sayles, who managed the small-cap fund. Norman promptly noticed Ben's ability to recognize growth trends and quickly identify stable investment quality funds. Ben kept it a nice and tidy fund taking it from a net worth of one hundred million to over one billion. Ben made life easy for investment managers all over the northeast, tracking the trends and informing them of good buys and hard sells. He also reviewed their orders and identified possible missteps so they could be corrected. He often averted embarrassing errors before they cost someone their job or they lost a valuable client. Ben was doing his overseer's position, leaving Norman a leisurely life of coffee and chitchat. When Norman retired, Mark, knowing Ben's skills, gave him his boss's job, since he was doing it anyway, and added bond acquisitions with a healthy raise.

Mark called Ben his golden boy, his tracking skills were unmatched, and Mark made regional director through his use of Ben's talents. Mark respected Ben and his ability and compensated him well with each of his promotions. They had a good working relationship. Frank, the head of security, was a retired NYPD detective. He was square-jawed with a crooked nose that must have been broken several times. He had a fit body with wrinkled, overly sun-exposed skin over taut muscles. He always wore short sleeve dress shirts that were a bit too tight. Ben assumed it was to accentuate his still pumped physique. He still had some of the Bronx in him and always had an entertaining war story to tell. He was the kind of guy you wanted on your side of a physical altercation.

"Good morning, Mark," Ben said.

"Not so good Ben, we have a big problem," he said in a concerned voice.

"A few days off and the bank falls apart?" he joked.

"Ben, we have some missing funds from the small cap," Mark said.

"How much and did you start tracking them yet?" Ben said as he moved to log onto his computer.

"Don't touch your computer. Take a step back," Frank commanded.

"Step back? What is going on, Mark?" Ben asked in a concerned tone.

"Yes, we tracked some of the funds to an account in the Canary Islands,' he added.

"I can get right on it. Did you check the account logs? I'll find out who is responsible. How much are we talking about?" Ben questioned.

"Ben, eight hundred and fifty thousand dollars are missing, and we did the digital logging. So far we found one hundred thousand in an account opened by you, and we're still looking for the rest," he said.

"Mine? Mark, what the hell are you talking about? It can't be mine; I don't have any offshore accounts and I sure as hell would not be stealing money from us," Ben stated emphatically. "Let me get on this. I'll get to the bottom of this," he said as he again moved towards the computer.

"Ben, we disabled your access yesterday, and as of then you are no longer employed by National," Mark said.

"You know I would never embezzle funds, Mark. You know me. How can you let me go without investigating?" Ben implored. As his words faded, two uniformed Hackensack officers walked in behind Mark and Frank with radios squawking.

"Ben, this is well beyond me already; from everything I have seen it all points to you," Mark said. "Sorry, Ben, it's a police matter from here forward."

Ben felt betrayed by his friend, his mentor. He was innocent, unjustly accused and headed for jail. The police handcuffed him and walked him out the front of the building to a waiting patrol car. Ben now knew the humiliation of a perp walk as he watched the expressions on the faces of friends and co-workers he was led through the office.

Ben's next humiliation was being processed at the local station. Mugshots, fingerprints, and unhappy faces everywhere; he received the full treatment. He was lucky it was early, and he was able to have his arraignment and was formally charged. The court set bail. The judge labeled Ben a flight risk because of the offshore account and made bail five hundred thousand dollars. Ben lamented, "I am now a flight risk, born and raised in northern New Jersey, educated Rutgers University, worked in Hackensack, and had my first out of the country trip to Aruba canceled due to lack of funds," he had to laugh. Ben called Sandy and explained how she needed to raise fifty thousand dollars to acquire a bail bond.

"Fifty thousand dollars? You're broke, and I'm not risking my money on a criminal," she told him.

"A criminal? Sandy, you're talking about me, you know," Ben said.

"I know who I'm talking about. I didn't realize I was dating a complete loser. I've had enough; get your own bail," she shouted.

"Sandy this isn't…." the line went dead before he could get his protest out. Ben informed the officer he had been disconnected. Ben was thankful he let him make another call. Ben tried to rationalize a reason why he maintained a relationship with Sandy. He no longer could find one.

Bail was a distant possibility, so he called a neighbor and asked her to look after Lucy and Melanie for a few days. She was a pleasant widow, and she loved the dogs. She always carried a treat for them in case she ran into them. She agreed, and Ben prayed it would only be a few days.

Chapter 53

Ben's heart dropped at the thought of not being there for his dogs. He was transferred to a holding cell where his mood continued to darken. There he sat, a caged animal. The cell had a cot, bolted to the floor, a bench seat, bolted to the wall, and what appeared to be a toilet, and it was a term he used lightly, sitting like a wart in one corner of the cell. An odiferous young man was sleeping in the cell next to his. From his appearance and scent, he was either homeless or was sleeping off an alcohol and drug binge. Ben felt the isolation and pain of confinement. He related it to how his Lucy and Melanie must have felt in the shelter they came from. How can anything, person or pet, tolerate this empty place?

Ben was informed that in the morning he would be transferred to a minimum security jail in Pine Plains. Wonderful. He tried to steel himself to the prospect of another jail; it may have worked if not for the knowledge his dogs would end up homeless again. The thought of losing his dogs was breaking him. From the day he rescued Lucy he knew he was her forever family. He never even considered he would be the one to mess up. Ben had lived every day since he adopted her feeling glad to get home to her warm greeting. He had a connection to Lucy he could not explain. Ben loved Melanie, but he has considered Lucy unique since the first time he laid eyes on her. He couldn't bear to break her heart. It was bad enough his heart was breaking. Ben's stomach churned with the thought of Lucy in a cold, loveless shelter. He saved her from the reality of the shelter and now he was going to fail in keeping his promise. He kept imaging the spark in her eye fading as time passed in the shelter. Ben felt his eyes watering up as he thought of his failure to Lucy. God, he knew he would be meat in here, a new inmate crying over a dog, what were his chances? He sat with his face in his hands; this was the point when men considered jailhouse suicide. In jail, with no hope, no future and the possibility of losing the one good and loving constant in one's life. It weighed heavily on his soul.

Ben sat in his self-made pit, growing ever deeper when a voice from beyond pulled him up.

"Mr. Grece, come; bail was posted, you can go."

The officer led Ben out to the front desk.

"How? Who?" They handed his belongings to him. From behind, Ben heard the voice of his boss,

Mark. "Ben, get yourself a good lawyer. I don't know what's going on in your life but you were always true to your word, and I feel I still owe you."

"Thank you," Ben said as tears ran down his cheeks. "For the record, I didn't do it. I can't explain what is happening in my life or why. I don't understand it myself."

Mark drove Ben to his car. Ben sat quietly watching the blocks pass. He reflected on the past events wondering how the current circumstances had transpired. Mark pulled beside Ben's car in the bank parking lot. Ben couldn't thank him enough. He swore to his boss he was set up. Ben had no idea who could do such things or why they would want to set him up.

"Mark I don't know how to…" he said as Mark interrupted

"Call us even, I can't help you any further without jeopardizing my position," he said. "Take care of yourself, Ben, I'm sorry for your trouble," Mark said as he pulled away.

"Not nearly as sorry as me," Ben thought.

Ben drove home, and as he pulled into his driveway; he could see Lucy and Melanie in the window. He was so grateful to be home and even more grateful to see Lucy. She greeted him with a full body wiggle and as he pet her saying, "Good girl, my good girl. Daddy's home," tears welled up again. He pondered, "What a baby I've become. I've cried more today than in my entire life."

Melanie pushed in for her scratch too. Ben put on the dog's leashes and walked, deep in thought about the recent problems his life had acquired. As he passed the McMansion, he saw Vic, the guy he had the dogfight with, walk out his front door to the edge of his driveway. Vic could not believe Ben was here walking his dogs as if nothing had happened. His sources told him that Ben had been arrested, yet here he was with that stupid look on his face. Sergio had forwarded the news of Ben's arrest to Manuel; Vic was expecting his payout, not Ben. This turn of events would reflect poorly with Manuel. Vic knew the possibility existed that he could end up on Manuel's short list. He composed himself as Ben drew closer. Vic gave a wry smile as Ben passed, and said,

"You don't look so good, my friend," and laughed.

"Excuse me, are we friends now?" Ben replied sarcastically.

"So are you sorry now?" he asked.

"I told you I was sorry," Ben said as he walked by.

"How is your job going?" he asked abruptly.

Ben turned and walked back.

"My job, why the interest in my job?" he asked with a growing suspicion this man was somehow tied to his recent bad luck.

"No interest, you just look a little beat up, is all," as he laughed again.

A light bulb lit in Ben's head with the realization Vic was somehow responsible for his misfortunes. He could barely believe a neighbor would do all this or even be able to cause the series of misfortunes that had befallen him. Ben wondered, "Why would someone go to such extremes over what started as a dogfight?" Ben knew he would never clear his name with a stealth opponent; he had to provoke Vic into tipping his hand. Ben had a bad feeling he was in for another beating.

"You think you're funny? If I find out you had anything to do with my problems, I'll give you another punch in the mouth," Ben said in anger.

"I wouldn't dirty my hands on you," Vic said spitting on the ground.

"That's what a coward says. If you have a problem with me, here I am, big man. What's the matter? You can't handle me?" Someone else was again speaking with Ben's voice.

The blood was pounding in his head; he shook with the frustration of knowing this man had everything to do with all his misfortune.

"Don't tempt me, I may just finish this myself," Vic said.

"Punks like you don't have the guts to face a real man. You're some kind of sick twisted punk. Was our fight the motivation for all this?" he blurted out. Lucy was getting nervous. Lucy started barking as Melanie pulled on her leash trying to escape the argument.

"I can squash pests like you and your dogs," Vic said.

"Small man, big talk; you know where to find us, if you can find your balls," Ben's voice said as he walked away.

"I'll finish this. I'll finish you," Vic blurted.

Ben turned to glare at him. Vic was red-faced and shaking. Ben guessed he got to him. Ben couldn't believe how he spoke to Vic; he thought it was awesome. He was standing his ground. He had enough. Vic watched Ben walk down the block. He burned with the thought "The piece of crap had the nerve to challenge me." He could see why Manuel wanted him dead. Manuel would pay Vic double if he killed Ben for him. Vic knew he and Sergio would have a problem if Manuel found out Vic screwed up and Ben was walking around a free man. Vic was also frustrated that his hacking of the stock fund was thwarted. He would give Sergio a call; Vic decided he wanted the money. He would take care of this pest himself and in the process earn the respect of Manuel Garcia. Even from jail, Manuel could make a man in this town. He watched his target walk around the corner with his dogs. Ben went home with Lucy and Melanie and checked every window and door. He slept with a baseball bat and one eye open. Ben told Lucy in the morning, "I'm going to see the chief; maybe he can help us."

Chapter 54

Once again Ben found himself sitting in the chief's office.

"Ben, I wish you were here on more favorable circumstances, I can't get involved in an active investigation; you know it's a conflict of interest. I could be jeopardizing my job and your position in the case."

"I guess you heard about my problem at the job then and, for the record, I'm being set up by someone. I don't wish to put you in a compromising position, but I have nowhere else to turn. Please hear me out; what I have to say may be my only chance to clear my name," Ben pleaded.

"If you cross the line here, I'm going to end the conversation, Ben," he replied.

"That's fair," Ben said.

Ben proceeded to tell the chief about his encounter with his neighbor. He told him about how a dogfight led to his fighting his neighbor. Ben told him how he tried to apologize and about his veiled threats.

"Chief, I think my neighbor Vic is somehow responsible for my run of problems," he said.

"It makes no sense someone would plan this elaborate set of circumstances over a dogfight. I think you're reading too much into this," the chief said.

"He knew about the problem with my job and the assault and made a point to tell me so," Ben said. "I did try to provoke him on our last encounter; I believe he'll try something again. He threatened he would finish what he started," he added. "You have to believe in me, chief. You know me well enough. I'm not a thief and how do you explain the assault, my bank accounts, and credit cards? It's crazy what has been happening to me. It has to be more than a coincidence," Ben implored.

"Ben, you've always been honest and upfront with me. I'll do what I can; my officers will run some extra patrols in the neighborhood, watch your back," the chief said. Ben knew the chief would do what he could; it made him feel a little better. He still could not shake off the weight tied to his life; he had an impending feeling of doom and wished he could shake it. Ben went home and kept all the blinds shut and walked the dogs in the yard. They ate and watched TV in the dark. Ben went through his window and door ritual before bed. He even let Lucy sleep on the bed next to his trusty baseball bat.

Chapter 55

Sergio met Vic at 1:00 in the morning. The surrounding homes were dark, and everyone would be asleep.

"Are you sure you want to do this, Vic?" Sergio questioned.

"Don't get squeamish on me now. We have a choice: tell Manuel we handled his problem for him and we'll make a few bucks, or have him pissed off at us because we failed. Manuel can put an end to our business or have us killed," Vic lectured.

"I don't like this; things are getting too intense," Sergio complained.

"Shut up, it'll get a lot more intense if Manuel thinks we let the dog guy get away with all this. C'mon, let's just get this done."

They walked around the block. Vic's heart was pounding in his chest. He never tried to kill a man and found the thought of it exhilarating. They approached Grece's house from the side yard. There was a large shrub shielding them from the street. They waited behind the bush making sure the house was quiet. There were no lights in the surrounding homes; it looked like they were good to go. Vic checked his gun, a Glock 26. It was a small nine millimeter automatic. Ironically, he bought it with Grece's credit card. It felt good in his hand. Their plan was to jimmy the basement lock again. Sergio had gained access to the house the same way the week before to give Ben his little lesson, one he apparently did not learn from. They were about to move when the beams of headlights turned onto the road. They stood in the shadows as a local patrol car passed the house. It was conspicuously slowing down as it passed Grece's house. Sergio was getting nervous; Vic grabbed his arm and whispered, "Hold still, he can't see us."

The patrol car passed and disappeared out of sight.

"I told you I don't like this," Sergio complained.

"Alright, we can come back later," Vic said.

They returned to Vic's house. Patrol cars came by on two more instances; Vic thought perhaps they were patrolling more frequently since Sergio beat Grece.

"Sergio, let's get some sleep. We can follow him in the morning. Hopefully, we can get him isolated," Vic said. They had time for a few hours of sleep.

Chapter 56

Ben woke from a restless night's sleep. He had nightmares that haunted him when he woke. He had lost his dogs and was searching deeper and deeper into a cave. The cave grew dark, and he could only hear the whimpering of Lucy as he crawled in the dark unable to find her. He woke in a pool of sweat with a feeling of dread.

He needed to get out and clear his head. He grabbed the dogs and jumped into the car and headed for their favorite hike, Ramapo Reservation. Ramapo was a great place to walk and hike with the Ramapo River running through it and two lakes. One lake was at the bottom of the mountain, and a cold stream fed another lake on the mountain. You had the choice of open semi-paved paths or rustic side trails winding through the Ramapo Mountains. You could walk for hours on some trails and not see another person for miles, or walk with groups of dog lovers taking their mutts to the upper lake to swim.

Vic woke Sergio early.

They had some coffee and parked their car down the road from Ben's house. They watched the house for an hour and a half when their patience paid off. Ben's car pulled out of his driveway.

"There he is, Vic, just like you said," Sergio said.

They pulled out and followed Ben at a distance. Ben stopped at Doing Donuts for coffee and a bagel for himself and a well-buttered croissant for Lucy and Melanie. Ben never noticed the duo following him. Vic and Sergio continued to follow the unsuspecting Ben. Ben pulled into the parking lot of Ramapo Reservation. There were already a fair number of cars in the large parking area. He parked close to the trail entrance and leashed his dogs. Sergio pulled next to a van shielding them from Ben. They watched as the trio stopped at a large rock that prevented vehicles from driving into the pedestrian path. Ben sat on the rock, and he and the dogs enjoyed their treats. When he finished his coffee, he told the dogs "Let's roll," and off they went.

Chapter 57

Ben and the dogs walked along the main trail. There were already other dog walkers and their owners on the main path. Vic and Sergio followed a safe distance trying to blend in with the other joggers and dog walkers. Ben crossed the main bridge over the Ramapo River. He had no patience for a crowd today, so he turned off the traveled path onto an excellent side trail. The trail snaked along the Ramapo River for a short stint and then turned up the side of the mountain. It was a moderately rustic trail and not very popular. He could let Lucy and Melanie run loose without disturbing other hikers. Lucy, with Melanie in tow, raced down the trail taking small detours to splash in the river before tearing through the brush in search of an unsuspecting squirrel or chipmunk. The trail meandered along the river for a mile before turning to the foot of the mountain. It led Ben and the dogs through a short patch of forest to a small bridge over a tributary feeding the Ramapo River. The trail then turned up past the crumbling stone foundation of a home of a time long past and up the mountainside. As Ben climbed the mountain trail, Lucy raced up the steep slopes, turned and deftly flew down again. Watching her always gave him a chill as she plunged without fear of finding footholds on the steep slopes. Melanie stuck to the trail trying to catch Lucy's attention with a nudge or a nip as she bounded by. It was a beautiful morning with bright sunshine. The forest was filled with hints of pine and an earthy leaf odor. Ben drew in deep breaths to cleanse his lungs. Down the side of the mountain, he could hear the rushing of a mountain brook that sat in the valley the mountain peaks created. As he meandered through the forested trail, his financial woes melted away. It was just him and his dogs and Mother Nature. Ben's spirits soared with each passing step. Far behind, two figures followed their unsuspecting victim. Ben was playing right into their hands.

Chapter 58

Ben was watching Lucy bound through the brush, thinking, "What's better than this?" when he heard the crack of a gunshot. "Hunters," he muttered to himself. He had heard their shots before, but this one was louder than usual. Crack, Ben heard a second shot and something flew off the tree next to him. He looked over and noticed a piece of the bark was gouged out. Ben turned to the direction of the sound. Lucy was crouched pointing in the same direction, she saw something. Ben saw a t-shirted man down trail move from behind a tree. He was wearing a black tee and black jeans. He could not make out the man's face at that distance with the shadows of the trees obscuring the light. Lucy moved towards the figure and let out a growl and then a bark. Crack, a third shot and something hit the trail by Lucy's front paw. "Holy shit," he thought, he was shooting at them.

Ben yelled "come" to Lucy and Melanie as he accelerated into a run up the trail. Lucy quickly passed him bounding ahead; this was a great game to her. Melanie was deathly afraid of fireworks, and with the last boom of the gun, she bolted in a panic down the side of the mountain before he could stop her. He watched her panicked flight as she tumbled and rolled down the mountain. Crack, there was a fourth shot. Ben heard the bullet pass through nearby brush. "Why is someone trying to kill me?" His mind came to one name, Vic, the psycho bent on destroying his life and who Ben believed had him beaten. He found himself sprinting up the trail. He had no time to get Melanie; he was relieved she was running away from his shooting attacker. Ben was running for his life. Vic and Sergio were toying with Ben. They closed ground on their intended victim. Vic knew he had him alone and isolated on a remote mountain path surrounded by dense woods.

Ben had nowhere to go. The path straightened out, and Ben knew here he would be an easy target. He turned and headed into the brush of the forest. Crack, another bullet whizzed past his ear. Ben in a panic screamed, "Lucy, come," for fear she may turn on his attacker and be shot. He ran wildly through the brush, thorns tore at his clothing and flesh, Ben's skin itched and hurt at the same time. His lungs burned, and heart pounded.

Vic was amused watching Ben's panicked run through the dense brush. He watched as he stumbled and fell trying to escape his fate. The rabbit darted off with no hole to hide. Vic mused, "I own him now. I'm the hunter and he's my prey."

He called to Sergio behind him, "Sergio, stay straight and cut him off from the front; I'll swing around and make sure he doesn't double back. Hold him for me if he runs into you. If I get him, you'll know. I'll put a bullet in his head."

Sergio ran ahead, and Vic swung around the backside of his panicked flight; the rabbit was about to be snared.

Ben could see Lucy deftly running beside him, skirting thorns and fallen branches as he clumsily stumbled and tripped over every obstacle. He looked back in a panic trying to see where the shooter was only to fall again. Ben wildly sought his feet. Ben's mind told him, "Keep moving or this nut will kill me here in the woods. IS this to be how my life is extinguished? On a back trail; found by scavengers and the flesh torn from my bones?" Another bramble tore his skin. He mused, "There'll be little flesh left if I continue this mad run through the woods." He was feeling lightheaded as his breath came harder; he imagined this was how a marathoner felt near the finish line. Ben's legs were becoming increasingly rubbery, his mind slipping into a state of euphoria as it was drained of oxygen. He looked to his side. There she was, his Lucy, dodging all the obstacles.

Her waving fur kept rhythm with her stride. Her tail straight back, flowing with the wind she created. Her tongue hung to the side of her mouth, and her breath was steady but not labored. Every muscle fired in unison and propelled her deftly forward. She was a miniature thoroughbred, muscles tuned, nostrils flaring, she could run for miles and not be exhausted.

"My Lucy, my beautiful Lucy," Ben said to himself with labored breath. She was a sight to see, a champion, the best in non-breeds. "Westminster, look out, here comes Lucy," he thought in his semi-euphoric state.

Ben, on the other hand, was struggling with his body, willing it to go onward. It answered with painful muscle cramps, aching joints, burning lungs, and a painful queasy feeling in his stomach. He was no thoroughbred! Lucy ran ahead of Ben, and at a full run, she suddenly stopped, turning back to look at him. He saw they were at a ridge.

Lucy was looking down from the top of a fifteen-foot drop.

Chapter 59

Ben pulled up beside her, bending over, his chest heaving for breath, his stomach asking permission to hurl his breakfast. The path was below. Ben felt a spark of hope that a path would lead him to people. He and Lucy had to keep ahead of this nut. Ben contemplated how they could possibly get out of this alive. He quickly lay down and, throwing his legs over the rocky ledge, Ben backed his body over and down the rock wall. He hung from the top with his fingers gripping the stone. Ben's feet flailed, feeling for a foothold. His legs were spastic and cramping from the run, reduced to useless appendages scraping aimlessly at the stone. His fingers ached, and his chest still heaved as he started to lose his grip. Ben was suspended for a moment. His mind found a split second of peace. His peace was abruptly interrupted by a slap from the ground. Ben's feet hit at an awkward, acute angle propelling him backward onto his buttocks. He felt electric shocks travel to the base of his skull. He tried to torque his body to prevent his head from whipping backward to the ground, taking the force of the path with the right arm and shoulder. Pain shot through his torso; his shoulder had not been right since the assault at the house. He felt now it must be shattered. Ben felt crunching and grating as he flattened out on the ground. He gasped for breath and fought back the pain. He would not allow himself to pass out, he had to get up and keep moving.

Ben willed himself to his feet. Pain shot out in a wild and chaotic dance throughout his body. His right shoulder had horrific pain; the arm hung down, spastic, unwilling to obey his brain's commands for fear of more pain. Ben looked up for Lucy, and she was at the edge of the rock cliff looking down concerned and restless as she sized up her predicament and looked for a way down. She would not try to find a path down for fear Ben would be out of her sight; instead, she jockeyed on the ledge contemplating where to jump. Whimpering for him, all he had to do was command her to jump, and she would fly into his outstretched arms. Ben lamented, "My arm is busted, but I need to save my baby."

"It's okay Lucy, follow me on the ridge, we'll find a place for you to get down, steady now," he commanded. As Ben turned to move, he heard the cocking of the gun and stood to face his attacker.

Chapter 60

Vic stood straight-armed with his gun pointing at Ben's face. Vic had circumvented the ridge, cutting off any escape.

"What do you and your mutt think now?" he asked.

"You're a madman, you're completely insane," Ben replied in a choking voice.

He just smiled. Ben's vision was distant, and the world seemed to be in a fog. His entire being hurt and for a moment he thought this must be a dream, no, not a dream, a nightmare. "This madman is going to kill me over a dogfight," ran through his head.

"What part of ruining my life wasn't enough for you?" Ben said in a failing voice.

"That was just for fun and profit," Vic replied, "I warned you not to mess with me. Don't you think I take care of my own problems? People like you think they can do whatever they want. You use and destroy everything in your path. Think again," he added.

Ben's mind was racing; he wondered if he could make a run for it, but he could barely move. He certainly could not expect to outrun a bullet. He could not rush him either if he could not move his arm. He heard a voice from down the path. "Vic?"

"Up here, Sergio," Vic replied.

From around the bend strode a sweating, well-built man in his early thirties. Ben immediately recognized him as the man who nearly beat him to death in his home. He must have seen the expression on Ben's face as he said, "Hello, Mr. Grece, so nice to see you again."

Ben's body shook at his greeting. Lucy started barking and whining louder with the appearance of another of their foes. She recognized him also. Ben ignored Sergio, keeping his eye on the gun in his face.

"You win," Ben stated. "You've taken everything I have; it must have been hilarious," he sniped. "How can you ruin someone so easily?"

"It's easy when it's your business; everything I need to know is just keystrokes away. It's stealing candy from babies. Most of the companies we steal from can't even be bothered to investigate; they just write off my spoils. The system is a joke made for people like me." Vic lectured.

"You're just another thief, Ben said.

"Perhaps," Vic added, "but as you'll learn, a thief not to be messed with. Now you'll see who is going to beat who."

"You did all this over a dogfight?" Ben asked.

"A dogfight?" Vic laughed. "You thought this was all about your stupid dog? You messed with Manuel Garcia. Are you so stupid that you don't know how connected Garcia is?"

"But he is in jail," Ben croaked out.

As Vic spoke, Lucy became very uneasy, scrambling along the edge of the rocks trying to find a place to jump. It was too high, and she whined and barked wildly as Vic delivered his manifesto to Ben. He rambled on about Ben messing with men like Manuel Garcia and himself; how Ben has made Vic become a killer; how he tried to have Ben jailed and let Garcia handle his own affairs but Ben's arrogant attitude pushed Vic to the edge. Ben would be responsible for his own death. Vic stated he was not the killer; instead, it was Ben who ultimately decided his own fate. Ben recognized Vic was genuinely paranoid bordering on insane. He tried to comprehend how Manuel Garcia, a drug dealer from Delaware, was able to orchestrate all this from a jail cell.

Ben asked, "So you work for Garcia?"

"I work for myself. Manuel asked me for a favor. I can see why he wants you dead," Vic scowled.

"He runs the jail, and Mr. Garcia asked me to take care of you. He put a contract out on your life.

I know you walk around with that stupid look on your face, but I now know you're as stupid as you look. You and your mutts are responsible for Garcia getting jail time. Did you seriously think that testifying against one of the country's most connected drug lords would have no consequences?"

"My testimony meant nothing; he was going to jail with or without my testimony," Ben said with a shaking voice.

"The fact is that your dog led the FBI right to Garcia; you and you alone are responsible for his time, so now he wants you dead."

"So you're his hit man?" Ben asked as a wave of fear passed through his body

"Hitman," Vic said with a laugh. "I'm not a killer. True, I may be a thief; I took this job just to get revenge for Mr. Garcia my way. I'm the one who now possesses your money, and you should be in jail right now."

"It was you who hacked the stock fund; you're the one who set me up with that offshore account."

"It was my pleasure to steal your money. I would've emptied the stock account, but someone stopped my masterpiece, perhaps it was you. You seem to have the dumbest luck of being in the wrong place at the right time; your being here instead of jail proves that. Manuel would be arranging a jailhouse accident for you and yet here you are forcing my hand."

"You're mad. I had no idea who stole the stock funds; no one is forcing you to do anything, I was lucky my boss bailed me out or perhaps I would be at the hands of Manuel," Ben said.

"Lucky, you're stupid; now I have to finish what I started. You and your mutts make me sick, you made me want to be a killer, and now I have had enough of you and your dogs. I'll earn the respect of Garcia, be well paid and not have to deal with you again. I guess your dumb luck led you here and now your luck has run out."

Lucy continued to bark through his rambling speech. Vic became perceptibly more agitated as he spoke.

"First, I'm going to shut your dog up," he bellowed.

Vic looked up at the whining dog, and when their eyes met, Lucy jumped.

Chapter 61

Ben watched Vic's arm twitch upward. His gun exploded, a flash and a deafening boom rang in Ben's ears as he felt the blast of heat from the gun's muzzle. Ben's head throbbed. He had instinctively closed his eyes wondering if he would feel any pain. Lucy slammed into Vic knocking him off his feet. Ben reopened his eyes, astonished to still be alive, in time to see Vic hitting the ground with Lucy on top of him. Ben lunged and fell on top of Vic's gun arm. With every ounce of strength he had left, he grabbed the gun.

Vic would not let go. Sergio reacted and started lunging toward them. Using his good left arm, Ben jerked the gun at Sergio. The gun reacted with another deafening boom. Ben was unsure how the gun had fired; his finger wasn't even on the trigger. Vic's finger still had possession of it.

A red spot appeared on Sergio's chest, he hovered for a moment with a confused look on his face before he fell to the ground. Ben held on to Vic's gun hand literally for his life. Vic pushed Lucy off him as he twisted and jerked his body around. Pain shot through Ben's body, as Vic rolled onto him. He felt his right shoulder crack, and pain flooded his body again. Ben felt vomit rise into the back of his throat. His ears rang, and the world started to spin and fade. Ben squeezed the gun thinking it would be a dead man's grip. He heard, "freeze," "freeze," as his mind began to shut down and he lost consciousness.

Ben felt himself shaking, someone was shaking him back to the world, "Try not to move, help is on the way," an apparition told him. His sight started clearing; Ben lay on the cold ground and the pain returned to him in waves. The apparition wore a hat and a badge. Ben looked down at his feet, and another ranger was holding Vic, his hands behind his back. Sergio lay on the side of the path near them.

"Lucy, Lucy," Ben muttered, "you saved me." Ben looked to his side, and there lay Lucy. "Lucy, here girl," he called weakly.

"Sir, keep your head still, try not to move," the officer instructed him.

"Lucy," Ben called.

She was not moving and lay completely motionless, her fur wet and flat.

"Lucy, what's wrong with Lucy?" he croaked.

Ben rolled towards her reaching with his uninjured arm.

"Lucy, please God, please, Lucy," he squeaked as he pulled his injured body to her.

"Please, sir, stay still, you're injuring yourself more," the officer cautioned.

He reached out again and touched her fur; she did not react. Her fur was clotting red blood.

"Sir, please …"

Ben interrupted, "No, you please, please help my Lucy."

He pulled her limp body to him and laid his head on hers.

He begged, "God, please, please don't take her. I need her."

Ben's eyes blurred, and he felt warm tears stream down his face. He felt sick, a sickness that seemed to darken his soul.

" I can't live without her. Please, God, you gave her to me to get me through all this, please don't take her now," he begged.

Ben turned to the officers, "She needs a doctor. Please, she saved me; don't let her die!"

He yelled to Vic, "You bastard, you shot my dog, you son of a bitch! Why, why would you do this?" he gagged on his words.

Vic laughed, saying, "You and that stupid mutt."

The officer holding him punched the laugh right out of him with a sharp blow to the stomach. Ben held his love as the blood formed a small pool on the ground; he found the wound and placed his hand on the hole.

"Lucy, Lucy," he sobbed as his entire being shook, "I knew from the day our eyes met we were to be together; please don't leave me now, I still need you," Ben could not stop the tears.

The medics arrived on an all-terrain vehicle. They ran to Ben as the officer informed them he was the victim.

"Sir, hold still," the medic commanded as he placed a blood pressure cuff on Ben's arm, trying to remove it from Lucy.

"Not me, Lucy. You have to help Lucy," Ben implored with every bit of breath he could muster. The medic tried pulling Ben's hand from Lucy; he resisted, clutching with every ounce of strength he had, sobbing uncontrollably, his tears mixed with his Lucy's blood. "Not me, you have to take Lucy, you have to save her, call Dr. LoFaro," he pleaded.

Ben refused their attempts to help him. He begged, crying over his furry love, until they promised they would take Lucy straight to the animal hospital.

"Her vet, Dr. LoFaro at the Emerson Animal Hospital, please get her there," he begged.

"We'll do everything we can to get your dog there. She's badly hurt, sir. I don't know if they can save her," the medic said in a somber tone.

"Please just get her there. It's the best chance she has; Dr. LoFaro will know what to do." Ben squeaked his words out as a wave of nausea overcame him. He felt the path spinning under his weight.

The medic lifted her gently. He put her in the rescue basket on the ATV. The medic quickly discussed it with his partner and the sheriff.

Ben blurted, "Take good care of her," as they drove off.

His partner called in, "Central, we have a shot canine in transport to Emerson Animal Hospital; contact a doctor LoFaro, the ETA is fifteen to twenty minutes."

The radio squawked back, "Canine, we copy, canine?"

"Yes, canine," he answered, "I'll update later."

He went on to request additional transport for the one human patient and one fatality. Ben watched Lucy round the bend; he could not remember any time in his life when he felt so alone and helpless. For the first time, he could not see a future with Lucy. Ben almost wished Vic had shot him too.

Chapter 62

They transported Ben off the mountain. It was a rough and bumpy ride on a modified ATV. It had an elongated back bed to accommodate a prone person. Ben, strapped to a backboard with a cervical collar in place, felt every stone and rut on the path. The vehicle listed as it maneuvered the rustic path and Ben felt as if both he and the vehicle would roll over. He worried about how Lucy handled the rough ride, she was hurt so badly. Once off the mountain, Ben could see the parking lot was full of a conclave of cars and trucks with lights flashing. More emergency vehicles than he had ever seen before. Chief Abraham stopped the medics from loading him into the waiting ambulance. Ben was shocked to see him there.

"Chief, my Lucy you have to..." the chief interrupted him.

"She's at Emerson. LoFaro has already brought her into surgery. He told me she's in real bad shape; she lost a lot of blood."

"I told you that guy was a nut, do you believe me now? He shot Lucy and tried to kill me."

"I did have some doubts, Ben, but I did some investigating. His desire to get revenge made him get sloppy; our cybercrimes unit was able to capitalize on his errors. National Bank was able to assist us in the theft of funds from your securities account, and we were able to establish there was a remote hack of your home computer. Homeland Security was able to trace some of the money trails. It led us to his accomplices, and I was able to place him on twenty-four-hour surveillance with the evidence we retrieved. We think he is the head of our state's largest identity theft ring. The FBI is executing over twenty warrants and making arrests as we speak. I owe you an apology for ever doubting your story."

"Vic told me Manuel Garcia ordered a hit on me; somehow he is involved in all this."

"Garcia, the drug lord's hand is in this? I should have suspected that this is too much of a coincidence. You testify, and a random dogfight sets a neighbor on you. It all makes sense now. Agent Freeman will be very interested in this. I'll make sure Garcia pays for this," the chief told him.

"Chief, you have to find Melanie. She ran when the shooting started, she must be lost on the mountain."

"Don't worry, Ben, there's law enforcement combing every inch of this mountain. I'll inform the rangers. I'll personally take care of her when they find her. I'll search these woods myself if that is what it takes to find her."

Ben with tears in his eyes thanked the chief. "You're a good friend," he said as they loaded him into the ambulance.

At the hospital, nurses and the ER doctor rushed to meet the incoming trauma victim. They cut away his clothing and started a thorough examination of his entire body. Amazingly Ben's shoulder was only dislocated and not fractured. With some mild sedation, which did not relieve any of his anxiety about Lucy and Melanie, they manipulated it back into its socket. The rest of him was a collection of scrapes and bruises. One young nurse commented it was the most she has ever seen on one person. All in all, he looked a lot worse than his actual injuries were. Ben's doctor wanted to admit him overnight for observation, but with a shoulder sling and a lot of apologies, Ben called a cab and signed out against medical advice.

He arrived at the animal hospital as Dr. LoFaro was leaving for home. Ben intercepted him as he was heading for his car.

"How is she, Doc? Is she going to make it?" Ben asked with tear-filled eyes. LoFaro told Ben that Lucy had a severed mesenteric artery and had lost a lot of blood. He explained he was unable to find any bowel perforations, but he could not be sure if he missed a small one. Her leg and ribs were also fractured in the fall. He told Ben it would be touch and go over the next few days. She was given plasma expanders, and he was able to get one unit of matching blood from the Oneida Animal Hospital. Dr. LoFaro had her in an induced coma on a ventilation assist device and antibiotics.

"The rest is up to her," as he grabbed Ben's good arm and hugged him as Ben sobbed uncontrollably.

"She has around the clock assistants monitoring her, go home and get some sleep," he said. "You can see her in the morning."

"Thank you. I know you gave her the best chance she has," Ben answered as he choked back his sobs. Ben watched as the doctor drove away. He sat on the front stairs of the hospital. He did not know how all his misfortunes would end. He sat, tears running down his face praying for the happy ending. He imagined if he could teach others one thing it would be: "If in your life you find the one animal you know was born just for you, love your pet as it loves you back. Saving a dog may also save you." He resigned himself to sit by his girl's side just as she sat by his as he reflected, "Yes, I love Lucy, and she loves me. I know now I didn't save Lucy, she saved me."

Chapter 63

As Ben sat on the cold front steps to the animal hospital, his mind kept wandering back to the dreadful thought his Lucy could die. His eyes watered up with the thought, and he found himself sobbing throughout the night. He dozed for short intervals and woke and cried again. Ben's heart was torn in half. He felt his world was empty without his dogs. The small sliver of hope Lucy would survive was all that held him to the world. The cold, desolate street was just another reminder of his isolation. He fell again into a pit of self-pity; its stone walls suffocated him. The heaviness grew in his chest as a knot formed in his stomach. On the other side of these walls was his love, fighting for her life, a cold, uncaring machine filling her lungs with the air she needed to live. Ben needed to see her, to feel her, to tell her he was there and he will be there forever. He envisioned Melanie scared and hungry, lost somewhere in the Ramapo Mountains. His girls were alone. In his world, alone was without him.

Daylight returned, and the sky brightened with hues of red and orange. The street sprang to life with motorists heading to work. Their lives continued. Ben's was on hold. Dr. LoFaro was the first to the animal hospital. He saw Ben as he pulled into the rear parking lot. Ben heard his car door close; Dr. LoFaro walked around the building to where he sat.

"Ben, my God, were you here all night?"

He tried to say yes, but he just started sobbing. Ben could not get his voice to answer. Dr. LoFaro hugged him.

"Pull yourself together, Ben. Let me buy you a cup of coffee; you look like you can use one."

"I'm okay," he answered in a broken voice. "Please, I need to see her. I need to see she's still alive."

"I spoke with my assistant earlier; she's hanging on. Come on. I'll let you spend some time with her."

Dr. LoFaro led him to his surgical recovery area. There, dwarfed by the machines keeping Lucy alive, was a small ball of black fur. She looked so lifeless, her chest and the substantial white gauze bandage on her belly moved with the hiss of the respirator. Tubes hung from her mouth, from her genitals and an IV tube snaked to her un-bandaged front leg. Dr. LoFaro explained the ventilator, the purpose of a catheter for urine and her need for fluids and anti-biotics. He hoped he could wean her off the respirator later in the day. He said time would tell if she was ready. Ben touched her greasy and dirty fur. It was already tangled and matted, and tears welled up again as he sobbed, inconsolable over his baby. If there was only something, he could do. His conscience told him this was his fault, and that made Ben cry harder. LoFaro hugged him again. Ben was coming unhinged with the guilt of his being the cause of Lucy's suffering and losing Melanie. It was tearing him apart.

"Ben, go home, get something to eat and some sleep. You can come back later to see her," LoFaro said.

"Okay," he sobbed back.

Ben thought to himself, "I have to stop crying, I need to get my emotions under control."

"Thank you for understanding," Ben said as the doctor led him out the door.

Ben had no intention of going home. He walked down the block to a coffee shop and had a bite to eat. He used the bathroom there and took a sink shower. Ben returned to his vigil and found a spot to sit along the side of the animal hospital. He sat watching the coming and going of dogs and cats of all shapes and sizes. He lamented how lucky they were to be with their pet even if it was sick. Ben wanted to get back in with Lucy, but he feared it might interfere with Dr. LoFaro. He did not want to alienate the doctor's goodwill. Ben waited until two o'clock and presented himself back to the receptionist. She escorted him to Lucy. He was glad LoFaro was busy, or he would have known Ben had never gone home. His disheveled appearance made it obvious. He sat with his baby until the assistant suggested he go home. Ben tried not to cry with little success.

Ben ate and used the facilities at the coffee shop again. He returned to his post on the side of the building and there he planned to sit and wait. Ben watched the staff leave one by one and saw Dr. LoFaro's car leave the hospital's parking lot. He was relieved the doctor did not see him. The veil of the night returned, with it his despair. Ben sat and blamed himself and prayed for his Lucy. A police cruiser pulled into the lot with headlights shining on him. Ben shielded his eyes from the glare as a figure appeared in the beam. He knew he was about to be rousted from his vigil.

"Ben, Dr. LoFaro called me; he suspected you would be here."

It was his friend, Chief Abraham.

"I need to be here," Ben answered.

"It's time to go home Ben," the chief said

"I know, I know," Ben said sobbing again. "You just don't understand how hard this is for me."

"I do, Ben, I've lost loved ones myself, but you still have a chance. Have faith and Lucy may come through this," the chief added. "Come on. It's time to go home. You need to eat and get some sleep. Lucy is in good hands. I can make some calls if you need to talk to someone professional or you can talk to me."

"You're a good friend, Chief. I'll be alright; thanks for the concern." He dried his eyes and realized he didn't even have his car. "Shit, my car is still at Ramapo Reservation," he told the chief.

"I had it towed to your house," he said as he put his arm around Ben's shoulders, "Get in, and I'll take you home."

Ben reluctantly moved to the police car. He approached the passenger side, and as his eyes accommodated to the light, he saw the fuzzy face of Melanie peering from the rear seat of the cruiser. It was difficult to tell who was happier. Ben cried as he repeated the words, "Melanie, Melanie, my baby," and Melanie produced a high-pitched whine and barking when she saw Ben.

"Chief, you found her!" he exclaimed as he opened the rear door of the car. Melanie jumped out knocking Ben to the ground as she washed his face between yips and whines. Ben lay there laughing as the tears continued to leak from his eyes.

"I would've told you they found her earlier today, but we couldn't find you. The rangers found her cowering in the old foundation on the mountain trail. They also found some shell casings farther along the trail; we assumed it was where the ambush began."

Ben was able to extricate himself from Melanie's affection and lifted himself from the ground as he thanked the chief for finding Melanie. For a moment he was happy again, but the moment passed as his thoughts returned to Lucy. Ben was coaxing Melanie into the cruiser's back seat when he noticed she had thrown up all over the upholstery.

"I'm sorry, chief. It looks like she threw up in your car. I'll clean it for you."

"Don't give it a thought," the chief said, "this is the second time she's thrown up in this car. She threw up in the ranger's truck, and she threw up in the Canine Units vehicle. We need to talk about what you're feeding her."

Ben smiled as he tried to wipe the vomit up with a receipt he had in his pocket.

Chapter 65

Ben returned daily. Lucy was taken off the respirator the following day. Her vital signs were excellent, and she had no fever. Dr. LoFaro felt her excellent physical condition before the injury favored her recovery. She was lifted from the drug coma and brought back to Ben on the eighth day when Dr. LoFaro felt she could be safely brought out of the coma. Ben watched teary-eyed as she awoke. She was weak, and he could see she was in pain. Her tail wagged ever so slightly when she saw him. He held her, sobbing again, and thanking God and the good doctor. He brought her home the following day. Ben was met by the chief, several officers, and his neighbors. They clapped and patted Ben on the back as he carried his precious Lucy into the house. She shook and whimpered with all the commotion, and he carried her to her pillow. Ben gingerly placed her on her bed cushion and covered her with her favorite blanket. They all were glad Lucy was alive. Ben, knowing Lucy was back home, was better too.

Vic had turned evidence on Manuel in an attempt to cut a deal for a reduced sentence and protection from Manuel's jailhouse justice. Manuel Garcia was transferred to a maximum security facility, shutting down his jailhouse syndicate. Agent Freeman turned up at Ben's door with an offer of protection in the FBI's witness relocation program. Ben was surprised when he answered the door and saw the agent. The agent wore a smartly tailored dark brown Armani suit with a light beige shirt and a brown and beige striped tie. Ben was impressed with how well the agent dressed.

"Agent Freeman, it's great to see you again and in a nice dry suit," Ben chuckled as he gave his greeting.

"It's nice to see you too and even better with no ocean around. How are those dogs of yours?" As the words left his mouth, Melanie bound past Ben covered in dirt and mud from her apparent digging in the yard. She jumped up on the agent in an enthusiastic greeting. Ben looked on horrified as he grabbed at Melanie and pulled her back. Agent Freeman looked at his soiled suit jacket and pants and as he brushed the soil off with his hand stated, "Some things don't change. That dog is unique."

Ben apologized profusely. He now owed the agent two new suits. The agent again told Ben not to worry. It was a part of the job.

"Come on in. I'll get you a washcloth and a cup of coffee," as Ben led the agent into the living room gesturing to the sofa. Freeman sat, and Melanie lumbered over, jumping on the couch next to him laying her dirty beard on his thigh.

"Oh God, NO, MELANIE GET DOWN," Ben said in a stern voice.

"It's okay, what can you do? I seem to have made a friend."

Lucy peered at the agent from the kitchen shaking and afraid to enter the room. Ben called the fearful dog as she cautiously came and jumped onto Ben's lap and stared at their visitor. Gazing at her shaved side with the large surgical scar, Agent Freeman asked.

"Is that the dog that was shot?"

"Yes," Ben answered.

"She appears to be doing well; Chief Abraham told me she was near death when it happened."

"Her wounds are healing, but I'm afraid her spirit is terrified," Ben added as he stroked his shivering dog. "I worry that she may never be the same again; the shooting took a lot out of her."

"I guess dogs are like people, emotional scars are worse than the physical ones," Freeman added.

"Lucy is an exceptional dog, and I often believe she is a person."

"Time heals all wounds; you and your dogs have been through a very traumatic crime."

The agent reviewed the witness protection program with Ben and offered to help him start over without worry about Vic or Manuel. Ben refused to leave his North Jersey home.

It was a long month of recovery for Lucy, and she was in so much pain. It continued to break Ben's heart. He could not help blaming himself. He regained his job. Mark, his boss, had Ben re-instated with a generous bonus and raise. Mark knew how Ben felt about his dogs and gave him all the time he needed to get Lucy well. Ben's life was back on track; now he had to get Lucy back. Her eyes were dull and lifeless. Her movements were tentative and guarded. She shook a lot, and it worsened with any loud noises or movements. The brush with death appeared to have damaged more than just her body.

Melanie took on the job of Lucy's rehab. Their roles reversed, and Melanie coddled, licked, and encouraged Lucy back to her former self. Ben was an observer and witness to the healing power of dogs. Time and Melanie healed Lucy's fears and anxiety, and as the two dogs healed, so did Ben's scars. Sandy had moved out, and Ben realized that he was better off alone than in a one-sided, loveless relationship. He hoped the day would come when he would find that loving woman, the soulmate, born for him. If not, he had his dogs, Lucy his canine soulmate and Melanie. Until that day he knew he was in good paws!

The End

About the Author

Bill Greco is a board-certified doctor of podiatric medicine. He graduated Fordham University and went on to earn his medical degree at the New York College of Podiatric Medicine in 1985. He currently works as a full-time clinician with the Hudson Valley Veterans Administration.

He is an enthusiastic volunteer in his community, having served as a councilman in his hometown of Montvale and is still a volunteer ambulance medic with the Triboro Volunteer Ambulance Corp. for the past twenty-five years. He is also a volunteer animal cruelty investigator with the Bergen County SPCA for the past six years.

Dr. Greco and his wife Laurie enjoy the love of their rescue dogs spending time with them between Montvale, New Jersey and Dewey Beach, Delaware.

Author's Note

Dear Reader.

I hope you enjoyed reading *Stumbling into Trouble* as much as I enjoyed writing it. Please do me a favor and write a review on Amazon. The reviews are important, and your support is greatly appreciated.

Thank you,

Bill Greco